JACK HAD NO JACK.
No job. No prospects. No hopes. No dreams. No beliefs.

HE OWED A LOT.
To Anne, for taking him into her life and her bed, so at least he knew where his next drink and night's sleep were coming from. And to Parry, who had even less than he, yet had enough to save him from being torched by fun-loving kids.

AND NOW IT WAS PAYBACK TIME.
Anne needed a man. Parry needed a woman. And somehow Jack, past master of the one-line put-down, had to cast his line to come up with both. . . .

THE FISHER KING

THE FISHER KING

A Novel by
Leonore Fleischer

Based on the
Motion Picture by
Richard LaGravenese

Ⓢ

A SIGNET BOOK

SIGNET
Published by the Penguin Group
Penguin Books USA Inc., 375 Hudson Street,
New York, New York 10014, U.S.A.
Penguin Books Ltd, 27 Wrights lane,
London W8 5TZ, England
Penguin Books Australia Ltd, Ringwood,
Victoria, Australia
Penguin Books Canada Ltd, 10 Alcorn Avenue,
Toronto, Ontario, Canada M4V 3B2
Penguin Books (N.Z.) Ltd, 182–190 Wairau Road,
Auckland 10, New Zealand

Penguin Books Ltd, Registered Offices:
Harmondsworth, Middlesex, England

First published by Signet,
an imprint of New American Library,
a division of Penguin Books USA Inc.

First Printing, September, 1991
10 9 8 7 6 5 4 3 2 1

PUBLISHER'S NOTE
This is a work of fiction. Names, characters, places, and incidents either are
the product of the author's imagination or are used fictitiously, and any resem-
blance to actual persons, living or dead, events, or locales is entirely coinci-
dental.

One

Everything you've ever heard about New York City—forget it. What they always feed you is lies. New York isn't a State of Mind, or a Wonderful Town, or the Big Apple, or the City That Never Sleeps, or any of the song lyrics or bullshit mythologies that are fed to a gullible public. Well, maybe the City That Never Sleeps is a fairly accurate description, because New York is not unlike the great white shark, endlessly circling, always awake, searching for prey, constantly on the attack. New York is a giant maw filled with many rows of serrated teeth, a territory devoted to kill-or-be-killed, you devour me or I devour you. You gotta be rich and clever to survive. If you happen to be one of the have-nots, then step back. Take a hike. Get lost. Ain't nobody come here lookin' for you, and we don't take messages.

On the other hand, if you're one of the haves, there's probably no more exciting place on earth to work or live than New York. It has everything—a glittering nightlife uptown and downtown, expensive shops, incredibly snobbish restaurants, the most exclusive hairdressers and couturiers, the best sex and the hottest music, the newest dances, the most beautiful women in the world, the most successful men. New York City is like the appetizer table at a Jewish wedding, loaded with salt and spice and cholesterol and flavor, with a waiter holding out pleasure in his right hand and indigestion in his left. If you've got the bucks, this burg has the bangs.

Fortunately for Jack Lucas, he was one of the haves, actually a supreme and shining example of a have. He personified You Are What You Own, Wear, Drive, Eat, You Are Where You Live, You Are Who You Sleep With, and—most important of all—Jack was a man whose own success he happily measured by the failure of others. The field of endeavor that had endowed him so richly with a good address, a gorgeous lover in her twenties, and other such hip worldly possessions was his own show on talk radio.

The *Jack Lucas Morning Show* was a smash success, the station's big leader. Jack had taken a moribund wake-up time slot on a moribund radio station and, using only his angry wit, his sharp talent for the spontaneous putdown, and his characteristically black outlook on life, had parlayed it into one of the most-listened-to programs on the air. Within a short time, he had become a cult personality with a large following. People tuned in to Jack with mingled curiosity and titillation just to listen to the feeble mews of the poor schlub Jack would be insulting next. In the bloody arena of talk radio, the listeners were the Romans, the callers were the hapless Christians, and Jack himself was the hungry lion.

Alone in his studio, he created a fantasy world for people who couldn't get themselves a life. At home or in their cars on the way to work, his audience couldn't see him, but they could imagine, through the rough masculine sound of his voice and the image of swaggering self-confidence he projected, that Jack Lucas was a superior kind of being who'd been handed the divine right to freely demean lesser beings.

From talk radio to insult radio wasn't really that much of a leap; Jack Lucas made it without straining a well-toned muscle. From insult radio to humiliation radio is a much longer stretch; even so, there were no beads of sweat on Jack Lucas's upper lip when he jumped over that barrier. As the clever centerpiece of one of Manhattan's most popular morning programs, Jack specialized in the humiliation and verbal annihilation of anybody dumb or desperate enough to call in. There were actually a surprisingly large number of wretched men and women who were so needy, so frantic to have their voices heard on the air, to have this master of stand-up contempt fling insults at their unprotected heads, that hundreds of them picked up their phones and literally invited their own belittlement, some on a regular basis.

For every sadist there's a whole bunch of eager masochists. Go figure.

So Jack Lucas, who viewed life from the bottom up, for whom the wineglass of life was perpetually half-empty, whose strongest emotion was discontent, managed to turn his pessimism into celebrity, his distaste for the human race into a large paycheck, the misfortunes of others into a plush life for himself, and all with the collusion of his victims. Hey, why not, this is the nineties, right? To make it in New York in the nineties, you've gotta have an edge, and Jack Lucas's edge was the carbon steel of impatience honed by the sharpening stone of egotism and held to the throat of a shivering humanity.

Strange, because he lacked neither intelligence nor education. Jack was a reader and a thinker. But since he'd become a cult figure and his fame and income had soared, somehow he'd lost the sense of the ridiculous he'd always had about himself and what he was doing. Ambition had put a halt to humorous self-examination.

His prime motivation was ambition, and what kept his ambition fueled was his lack of involvement with anybody but himself. Jack Lucas kept a comfortable distance from and a patronizing attitude toward every other life-form on the planet. His soul, or what passed for his soul, was housed in a glass isolation booth, for which his little broadcast studio was the perfect metaphor. His listeners could hear him, but they could not see him; above all, they could not touch him. All in all, not a very nice guy, but a very successful one. As Jack himself would say, "Fuck nice."

Jack had been nice once; when he was a young man, his deep-set blue eyes had beamed whenever his wide mouth had broken into a broad grin. There was a time when the expression on his handsome face hadn't yet hardened into a permanent sulky, bored grimace with turned-down lips. Once upon a time he'd even had a few ideals, one or two youthful altruistic impulses to maybe make the world a little better than he'd found it. So what had happened to change him?

Years had gone by and Jack didn't see the world getting any better. In fact, it got a helluva lot worse, and no effort of his seemed to make any difference. Maybe it was the greed of the eighties, that me-first decade of junk bonds and junk people. The trash track can be very seductive when you're running on it. It doesn't like to let go. Maybe because life itself had laughed at Jack more than a couple of times—it made him swear to have the first laugh from now on. Maybe it was the fact that never, in all his forty-one years, had he found another human being to love, really love.

There were girls, of course; oh, my God, yes! There was an apparently endless procession of beautiful women parading through Jack Lucas's life— models, actresses, even writers and painters, if they were gorgeous enough, if their legs were long, their thighs were narrow, and their butts as round as

MacIntosh apples. But although they touched his body, they hadn't touched his heart.

Now, at forty-one, where was his heart? Certainly not where you could get near it, or even where Jack himself was conscious of its existence. Jack had attained just about everything he wanted—fame, money, a great pad overlooking Manhattan from three directions, an apple-butt girlfriend. He traveled by stretch limo with one-way glass windows, he wore Italian designer suits at nineteen hundred dollars a pop; his feet sported custom-made three-thousand-dollar snakeskin boots with silver tips, cold-blooded creatures. If he couldn't feel joy, well, who the hell needs joy? Jack Lucas wasn't feeling pain, either. And that was about all you could ask for in this crummy world. No pain.

Yet, as popular as his radio program was—and it had captured the morning drive-time audience—he was finally getting bored with it. Getting out of bed at four to wake up the yahoos and morons of the five boroughs at six A.M. was no longer his idea of bliss. It was time to move upward and onward.

But his career seemed to have stalled right here, in this small studio, too hot in the summer and too cold in the winter, smelling of stale cigarette smoke, with the "On Air" sign flashing and the phone buttons lighting up. If the broadcast studio kept the world locked out, it also served to keep Jack locked in. That made Jack Lucas feel even more bitter, and his bitterness poured out like toxic waste all over the poor defenseless assholes who called in to his board.

Most of Jack's callers were kookaburras, of course, because the kookier they were, the easier it was to attack them and the more laughs his attacks won for him; the more laughs, the more ratings. These men and women were the ones desperate to let the world know they'd spotted UFOs, or were being followed by the IRS or the phone company, or they had the real skinny on exactly which section of the West Side Highway Jimmy Hoffa's bones were cemented into. Jack would string them along for a little while, let them get their weirdness across to the audience, and then . . . crash! He'd pull the rug out from under them and send them tumbling back down into the vortex of near madness from which they'd sprung.

Jack Lucas's equipment was minimal—a wicked wit, a microphone, a broadcast booth, a couple of sound engineers, and a rack of tapes that held an assortment of bizarre noises. The tapes were sound effects of cheers, and boos, and "awwwws," and corny inspirational music, and any other effect that enhanced the humiliation of the caller. Jack could put his hands on any tape at any given moment, slap it into his control board, and it sounded instantly like a large studio audience was backing up his insults with heckling cheers and jeers.

"Hi, this is Monday morning, and I'm Jack Lucas, and we're discussing personal pet peeves. You're on the air, caller."

"Okay," said an uncertain and fluttery female voice. "Well, it's my husband."

"Uh-huh," Jack answered encouragingly, but he glanced at his Rolex, wishing he could make time move by pushing the hands of his watch around the dial.

"He drives me crazy!" the woman complained. "I'll be talking and he'll never let me finish a sentence. He's always finishing my—"

"Finishing your thoughts," said Jack wickedly. "That's awful."

"Oh, it absolutely drives me—"

"Drives you crazy, huh?" Jack beat her to the end of her sentence. "He's a scoundrel."

"Jack, you hit the nail on the head." His caller sighed.

"Yeah? Well, somebody ought to hit you on the head." He pressed the next phone button, cutting off not only her next sentence but her call. In the control booth, the engineers snickered.

Although he relied on callers to keep the ball rolling, from time to time Jack Lucas actually sought out his own victims. As, for instance, now, when he was hassling on-air the female half of the most recent Washington sex scandal, a young woman whose unlisted telephone number Jack had obtained through a clever bit of bribery.

". . . This is disgusting. I don't have to talk to you," the girl was saying resentfully. It was a good connection; every nuance of her ashamed unhappiness would be clear to the audience.

"Yes, yes, you do," responded Jack, reaching for one of his tapes, "because you see, today you're our—"

"Spotlight Celebrity" echoed from the tape. The home audience sat up and took notice. Spotlight Celebrities were a sensational highlight of every show.

"And in the spirit of fairness," Jack continued, with nasty glee, "we want the public to hear your side of things. So, now, how long were you and Senator Payton having this sleazy affair?" He was rewarded by guffaws from the engineers' booth.

The young woman bridled, her voice thick with indignation over the telephone. "I'm sick and tired of the public thinking they've got the right to invade a person's private life."

"Oh, please!" Jack scoffed, heavy sarcasm dripping from every word. "You had sex with a United States senator in the parking lot of Sea World! You're telling me now that you're a private kind of person? No, you're our—"

"Spotlight Celebrity!" The tape again.

"That's still all anybody talks about." The young

woman sighed sadly. "Nobody even thinks to ask whether we loved each other."

"Because nobody cares about that, sweetheart. Nobody wants to hear about your romantic love. No, we want to hear about the backseats of limos . . . the ruined lives of people we want to be . . . new and exotic uses for champagne corks—"

"Listen, I've been humiliated enough already!" She was becoming really angry under Jack's eager probing.

"Perhaps not." Jack grinned. "We need those details!"

But no details would be forthcoming. With a snarled, "You're a pig, Jack," the young woman had broken the connection by slamming down her receiver. Jack laughed out loud in disparagement and pressed down another one of his phone's lit buttons.

Please, God, let the next caller not be so fucking boring! Jack prayed silently. Let's get a little action going. I'm dying in here! Just give me some lamb-o I can sink my teeth into!

"Hello, Jack, it's Edwin."

"It's Edwin!" The answer to his prayer, in spades. Jack greeted him joyfully, and in the sound booth the engineers cheered. Edwin Malnick was one of the program's regulars, another big loser at the game of life, always good for a few laughs. Jack slapped in a fanfare tape, and a swell of music announced Edwin.

"Edwin, we haven't heard from you in, what, a day? I've missed you." The poor schmuck couldn't afford a shrink, but he looked on Jack Lucas as some kind of benevolent God of Good Advice.

"I've missed you, too, Jack."

The "Awwww!" tape was appropriate here.

"So, Edwin, baby, this is Sunrise Confession time. What have you got for us?"

"I . . . I went to this bar . . . this very, ya know,

hard-to-get-into place, called Babbitt's,'' the man's voice began shyly.

"Yeah, I know the place.'' Jack grinned, and his grin was tinged with malice. "It's one of those chic yuppie gathering holes.''

"Uh, okay, I know, but . . . I met this beautiful girl.''

Music welled from the south booth, drenching the airwaves with syrupy lyrics. "Goin' to the chapel, and we're gonna get maa-aried. . . . ''

"Now, Edwin''—Jack laughed—"if you start telling me you're in love again, I'm going to have to remind you of the time we made you propose to that checkout girl at Thrifty's that you liked so much. Remember her reaction?''

Jack slipped the "AAAAArrrrrggggghhhhh!'' sound tape in swiftly and then choked off the scream. It was a great effect, one of his favorites.

"I wasn't serious about her, Jack,'' Edwin answered defensively. "That was just a joke for you guys. She was just a girl. This is a beautiful woman.''

Jack Lucas had a momentary visual flash on the caller, drippy Edwin Malnick, even though he'd never seen him. He could picture pale thinning hair, a large Adam's apple, and protruding ears that went red with embarrassment, weak blue eyes behind thick glasses, knobby knuckles. A virgin, he'd swear to it, the kind of dimwit that even the most desperate old maid wouldn't go out with. What a loser!

Edwin continued, unfazed, just happy to have Jack's attention. "I think she likes me. She gave me her number. But she must work a lot, 'cause when I call she's never home. But I think we'll go out this weekend. I've—''

"Yeah, Edwin, sure, and Pinocchio is a true story,'' Jack interrupted harshly, his patience at an end. This hopeless asshole was a complete cipher;

he would never, never have any effect on anybody's life. Jack felt he'd strung the nerd along long enough; time to lower the boom. "Edwin, wake up! This is a fairy tale!"

"No, Jack," protested the caller, his voice going thick as his defensiveness grew. "No, it's not . . . she likes me!"

"She gave you the old brusheroo, kiddo," Jack scoffed into the microphone as he reached for his cigarettes. "Believe me, this tart will never make it to your dessert plate." He snickered a little at his own wit.

"She likes me, Jack." Edwin was stung, but he came bobbing up for more. "She said for me to call."

Lighting up, Jack Lucas drew the harsh smoke deeply into his lungs. "Edwin . . . hey, c'mon, Edwin . . . Edwin . . . I told you about these people," he said with phony cameraderie. "They only mate with their own kind. It's called yuppie inbreeding. That's why so many of them are retarded and wear the same clothes. They're not human. They can't feel love. They can only negotiate love *moments*. They're evil, Edwin. They're repulsed by imperfection and horrified by the banal, everything America stands for. Everything that you and I fight for." Jack warmed to his topic, allowing the bile of his own prejudices to wash mockingly over his listeners. He had absolutely no grasp of what effect his words might have on others; all of Jack Lucas's thinking was one-way, like the window glass in the studio limousine that took him everywhere. He could look out, but nobody else could look in. "Edwin, they have to be stopped before it's too late. It's us or them."

There was a brief silence while Jack's words sank in, then Edwin said quietly, "All right," and hung up.

Jack Lucas's lips twisted in a sneer and he ground his cigarette out in the already-filled ashtray. Edwin Malnick! Quel dork!

The morning dragged on, with crank call after crank call, with every variety of dingbat and moron the city could provide from its overflowing coffers of lunacy. The hands of Jack's criminally expensive wristwatch crept with tortured slowness around its face, and the large studio clock with its sweep second hand taunted him at the same molasses pace. And yet, time did in fact pass away, minute by agonizing minute, until it was time for sign-off. The next slot would be filled by encapsulated headline news and ten minutes of weather and traffic, then the next talk-radio host, a fat, genial robust fellow whose idol was Arthur Godfrey.

"Well, folks, it's been a thrill, as always. Have a perfect day. Everyone here on the *Jack Lucas Morning Show* says 'bye." Jack ground out the last cigarette butt and threw the empty pack on the floor. His throat was a little sore; he'd have to start cutting down.

"This is Jack Lucas . . . so long . . . *arrivederc* . . . I'll be sure to send you a thought today as I lie in the backseat of my stretch limo, having sex with the teenager of my choice. And that thought will be—thank God I'm me!"

TWO

"You know, some of this is very funny." Lou Rosen chuckled, waving the script of the pilot of a new TV sitcom, *On the Radio,* at Jack. Lou Rosen was Jack Lucas's talent agent, from one of the two most high-powered agencies. Jack might be one of his smallest clients at present, but he was up-and-coming, and ambitious, so Rosen coddled him. "Cheever told me they've even secured the rights to the Donna Summer song to play over the credits."

"Ooooh, I have chills," Jack replied sourly, but his sarcasm bounced right off the professionally ebullient Rosen. "Are you sure they want me?" he continued. "I won't read it unless I have an offer."

Lou Rosen looked sharply at his client. They were all the same, performers. Babies, toddlers. All of them neurotically insecure, all demanding to have their nervous little hands held. In his best fifteen-percenter tones of reassurance, he said smoothly, "Jack, of course. Not even a question. When I spoke to him on the phone this morning, I could actually smell how much they want you for it. I could smell it over the phone." He made a little sniffing grimace to demonstrate, and it seemed to Jack that between his large round eyes, small balding head, and twitching nose, the agent looked like a cross between Bugs Bunny and Elmer Fudd.

The pair were seated in the spacious back of the stretch limousine the station had put at Jack's disposal. It was the ultimate status symbol—a city-block long, with a wet bar and TV in the back, one-way glass windows, the latest magazines and fresh newspapers in the door pockets, and the driver even wore a cap. It was Jack's pride and joy; he loved his limo with a passion, although he was too cool to say so out loud. He was always Joe Cool, as though the car and driver and all his other status symbols were just things, only possessions about which he couldn't care less.

Now the limo stopped at a traffic light. A street bum, unwashed and ragged, shambled over hopefully to the limo, tapping with filthy fingers on the one-way glass, trying to peer in. Lou fumbled in his jacket pockets. "I don't think I have any change," he said apologetically to Jack.

Jack glared at his agent through his costly Vuarnet sunglasses. "I am not opening this window," he snapped. "A couple of quarters isn't going to make any difference anyway." He had no idea how the future was waiting to make him pay for those words.

The light changed and the limo pulled away into traffic, as sleek and polished as a rifle bullet. The have-not panhandler looked after it sadly, too wretched, too forlorn even to be angry.

For an apartment to rent for $4,500 a month it has to offer extras, even in midtown Manhattan. Jack's apartment had lots of extras. It was a two-bedroom duplex in a brand-new building, at a good address. Ceilings were higher than usual, and the closets were generous. The space was vast; the living-room windows were two stories high, the view unobstructed on three sides. In the second bedroom Jack Lucas had created his own private playground, a media room cum gym, with state-of-the-art sound and visuals and the ultimate fitness equipment. If a man is known by the price of his toys, then Jack Lucas must be famous indeed, because his toys had set him back many tens of thousands of dollars.

Coffee. He had to have coffee. Jack walked over the expensive Pirelli industrial rubber tiles imported from Italy, picked up an expensive stainless-steel kettle designed by architect Michael Graves, and took it to the kitchen sink to fill. As the water splashed into the kettle he scowled. There was black ink in the sink again. If he'd told her to be careful once, he must have told the bitch a thousand times. . . . Angrily, he rubbed the ink off with paper towel, squinting to make certain that no black stains remained, and flushed the water down the drain.

Carrying the kettle to the stove, he stared into it, checking out his reflection in the shiny steel, and the scowl deepened. "I hate my cheeks," he growled, his customary discontent eating at him.

Jack slammed the kettle onto the burner and stalked angrily into the dining room, where Sondra, his live-in girlfriend, was sitting at the table, sketch pad open, making careful ink drawings of the oat-bran box, drawings she would later embellish with genitalia. Jack couldn't figure it, but the girl was represented by a fairly well-known art gallery, and she actually did sell some of her work, weird as it was.

Sondra's firm body, as narrow as a splinter, still fascinated him, although he'd long ago lost interest in anything she had to say. Life would be so great for him if Sondra would only keep her legs open and her mouth shut.

"Can I just ask that when you clean your hands, you wipe the ink off the inside of the sink before it stains the porcelain?"

"You can ask," Sondra answered with indifference, not bothering to look up. Six months of living with Jack Lucas and his constant pickiness had inured her to his litany of petty complaints.

"Raoul called before. About dinner," the girl added listlessly.

"About dinner as a concept or about dinner with . . . Raoul?" Jack replied with no real interest in the answer.

"You're so witty. I'm so jealous," said Sondra tonelessly, bored. "I need to get out of here, Jack, and do something other than sit in this apartment and count how many funny lines you have per page."

Jack glared at her. "You know, tomorrow's a very big day for me," he said petulantly. "It would be nice if you pretended like you understood."

"Fine. I'll say no."

"They're putting me on film tomorrow." He was still hoping for some encouragement, a little praise, a reaction of some kind. Fat chance. This relationship had run its course, and all it needed now was to be put out of its misery. If only she didn't have such a tight bod. If it hadn't been for the shape of her ass, Sondra would have been out on it weeks ago.

"Fine!"

"For the first time in my life I'll be a voice with a body. Do you know what that means? What this could lead to?"

"It's a sitcom, Jack, you're not defining Pi."

"I'll remember that the next time you get excited by drawing pubic hairs on oat bran," he snapped back sarcastically. Going to the bookshelf, he removed a copy of Albert Camus's *The Stranger,* and pulled out his stash of sensamilla. Sitting down on one of the Le Corbusier cube chairs, he quickly and neatly rolled a generous joint. He lit it and offered it to Sondra. "Want some?"

"No, I have to work."

Jack toked deeply, held the smoke right down in his lungs, and exhaling at last, answered, "How unsixties of you."

"I was nine years old in the sixties," Sondra reminded him with relish.

As the high began to kick in, Jack stood up and strolled to the window, staring without seeing at the city spread out twenty-nine stories below him. He was caught up now in his own vainglorious fantasy. "I used to think my biography ought to be entitled *Jack Lucas: The Face Behind the Voice*," he mused. "But now it can be *Jack Lucas: The Face and the Voice* . . . or maybe . . . just *Jack!* Exclamation point."

He waited for Sondra to say something, but the girl, self-absorbed as usual, didn't appear to be listening. She headed up the stairs to the bedroom above, unbuttoning her blouse as she went. Jack looked up just as she'd shed the blouse. The sight of her small, uptilted breasts gave him an immediate hard-on, and he followed her up the stairs and into the bathroom, where Sondra, now naked, had just turned on the shower and was fiddling with the taps to get the water temperature right.

As she stepped inside, Jack shucked off his pants and shirt and followed her.

"Can't we do this later?" Sondra whined. Then, as Jack's hands busied themselves with her wet body, she grudgingly began to give in. But what was in it for her?

"All right . . . okay. But if we do this now, can I have dinner with Raoul?" Sondra wheedled, knowing she had him by the short and curlies.

Jack grunted his assent, and so another yuppie love moment was negotiated.

Afterward, carrying the other half of the joint and a couple of fingers of good bourbon in a Steuben glass, Jack took the script and some takeout Hunan food into the Jacuzzi with him. "Hey, forgive me!" he practiced while soaking in the tub. He kept trying different readings, looking for the one interpretation that would capture the producer's attention and win him the audition, the reading that would crack everybody up. This could be the tag line that would make him really famous, like Ralph Kramden's "To the moon, Alice!" or Jack Benny's "Welll!" or Fonzie's "Ayyyy!" or Archie Bunker's "Stifle y'self, Edith!" or John Belushi's, "But NOOOO!" Memorable comedy lines like those really had an impact on a TV audience. One good catch phrase could catapult an ordinary man into the stratosphere virtually overnight.

"Hey, for . . . give me! Hey, *forgive* me! Hey, FORGIVE me! Hey, forgive ME! Hey, forgiiiive ME! HEY! Forgive . . . MEEE!"

Each interpretation pleased him better than the last. He could do this. He was really getting a handle on this thing. "HEY . . . FORGIVE ME!" Yeah, that one was really good. He'd go with that reading at his audition for *On the Radio* tomorrow, knock them all dead. They wouldn't be able to turn him down. It would be a lock. He'd be on his way, out of the hellhole of early-morning radio.

"I have this, I really have this!" Jack gloated to himself. "My life is really about to change!"

With a towel wrapped around his waist, he strolled into his den, his private sanctuary. This was the room that contained his Sharper Image toys, audio and video on the cutting edge, his in-wall speakers, his compact disks, his laser-disk projection system, his twin VCRs, his media wall with three television monitors, each screen tuned to a different channel. The sets were all on, but the sound was on mute. Jack loved that, three screens in action with no sound. It gave him a real sense of power to control all their voices, to let the screens speak or not speak, to play God with them.

As he rubbed his long hair dry Jack scanned the

screens idly. Nothing happening. Just the eleven o'clock news, a collection of earnest men and women with perfect hairdos sitting at news desks mouthing silence. Still a little high, he clicked the remote control and changed all the channels until all sets tuned to the same picture.

Jack was about to turn away when, suddenly, his eye was caught by the sight of his own face up there, in triplicate, like an Andy Warhol silkscreen. Inexplicably, surprisingly, there he was—Jack Lucas, on the eleven o'clock news. What the fuck? Quickly, he grabbed up the remote, turning on the sound.

". . . Everything America stands for. Everything you and I fight for. Edwin, they have to be stopped before it's too late. It's us or them." It was his own voice Jack heard, his words from this morning's show, followed by the solemn voice of the broadcaster.

"We go to a live report from Marc Saffron at the scene."

Channel 10's ace city reporter was shown looking solemnly into the camera. "It was Mr. Lucas's offhand remark that seemed to have a fatal impact on Mr. Malnick. An after-work hot spot, Babbitt's is popular with single young professionals." Behind the reporter, the camera pulled back to show the exterior of Babbitt's, an attractive watering hole on New York's trendy upper east side, all stained-glass hanging lamps and lush green plants and a twenty-foot-long mahogany bar. "Edwin Malnick," Saffron continued in his deepest tones of serious newscaster, "arrived at the peak hour of seven-thirty, took one long look at the handsome collection of the city's best and brightest, then removed a shotgun from his overcoat and opened fire."

What did he say? *What the fuck was the man saying?*

Appalled, Jack could only stare at his media wall

in disbelief. His nice warm buzz had evaporated totally, and he was stone sober. Every word of the newscast, every graphic visual, imprinted itself on his brain.

What he saw was a scene out of hell. The screen was filled now with an interior pan of the bar. Black zippered body bags were being carried out, and paramedics were wheeling out gurneys on which a few wounded people still clung to the last remnants of existence. Ambulances stood by, their colored lights rotating, casting weird flickering shadows over the scene.

Jack saw men and women sobbing; a few still screamed in fear as medical workers helped them out of the bar. There was broken glass and blood everywhere; it looked like a war zone—Beirut or Baghdad. It wasn't real; it couldn't possibly be real.

"Fuck," Jack whispered through dry lips.

The news story continued dispassionately. "Seven people were killed before Malnick turned the gun on himself and shot a hole through his head."

Without realizing it, Jack sank into a chair with a small moan. His eyes remained glued in horror to the screens. "Representatives of radio cult personality Jack Lucas expressed regret; however, no formal comment has been made. Neighbors of Edwin Malnick said he was a quiet man who lived alone. 'You scarcely knew he was there,' said a woman who lived next door to Malnick for eleven years. But tonight, few will soon forget this lonely man, who reached out to a world he knew only through the radio . . . looking for friendship . . . and finding only pain . . . and tragedy. . . ."

"This is Marc Saffron . . . Channel Ten News," said the broadcaster, and the channel cut to commercial.

Jack's shock dwindled away, turning to disbelief, then denial, then finally, acceptance, a certainty mingled with horror. This is my fault, he thought, my fault. I did this. Seven dead. Seven dead, and Edwin makes eight. Every word was another nail hammered into the coffin of Jack Lucas's pampered life.

For forty years Jack had chosen not to live, but to skate, like some weightless water bug, on the surface tension of life, never actually getting his feet wet. Now that meniscus was suddenly torn, and he was plunged deeply below the surface, where there was no oxygen. He was drowning.

Jack sat frozen as a dozen different screens chattered on with the latest claims made by an oven cleaner; he couldn't move, he couldn't speak. Within the handful of minutes the news item had taken, Jack Lucas's life had changed finally and forever. The old life disappeared as though it never was; the new life was unspeakable to contemplate. As his telephone began to ring and ring and ring, the comfortably padded isolation booth of Jack Lucas's soul shattered into a million brittle fragments. Like the Angel Lucifer expelled from heaven, he went plunging down, down, down, spiraling headfirst into the yawning bottomless pit of earthly despair.

Three

Any big city anywhere in the world is exactly like a rotted-out hollow log. It may appear clean and dry on top, but if you kick it over, you'll see blind, white, crawly things slithering out from underneath. These faceless creatures creep away hurriedly, rushing to get out of the painful light. In the last eighteen months since the senseless multiple murders at Babbitt's, Jack Lucas had become one of those scurrying creatures.

Six city blocks west of Jack Lucas's high rise and sixty thousand light-years away is Eighth Avenue. Hooker heaven, druggie delight, it's where runaway children go to earn the price of a meal with their own degradation. At night, Eighth Avenue is home to garbage, overflowing cans of decaying former food, picked over in alleyways by scrawny, starving cats. Human garbage, too, the dregs of life, scuffling and shuffling from one side street to the next in search of the next trick, the next meal, the next fix. Hope for the hopeless.

By the light of day it was only a little better, triple-X-rated porno houses, straight and gay, stood cheek by jowl with small bodegas run by local Hispanics, newspaper stores that sold more lottery tickets and cigarettes than papers and magazines, and Chinese-Cuban restaurants advertising *comidas y criollas*. During the day lunchtime crowds from the nearby office buildings on Seventh and Sixth felt safer venturing onto Eighth to buy a cheap hot meal, browse in a bookstore, rent a video.

"Those people are insane today." Anne Napolitano sighed, coming into the tiny back room that served as her office. "They took insane pills." She waited for Jack to answer her, but Jack said nothing, immersed as usual in a sleazy tabloid he'd picked up at the checkout line of the local superette. He sat with his feet up on Anne's desk, a lit cigarette in one hand, a bottle of Jack Daniel's conveniently standing by.

Anne raised her voice impatiently. "Hey, Mr. Happiness!"

Jack lowered the paper. In the year and a half or so since the shootings at Babbitt's, Jack Lucas had become a changed man. He even looked different, older, thicker, bloated, unshaven, his eyes red-rimmed and bleary. He looked like a man who viewed the world from the bottom of a whiskey glass, and the bottle of bourbon that stood close to his reach confirmed it. He didn't have the job anymore; the *Jack Lucas Morning Show* was history, toast. Gone, too, were the chauffered limo, the fancy apartment, the designer marijuana, the tight-bodied girlfriend, all toast. Swept away. Gone was every vestige of his pampered former life—except one. Somehow Jack Lucas had managed to hold on to one remnant of his glittery past. He still wore the custom-made snakeskin boots with the solid silver fittings. Of course, the boots, like Jack himself, had seen much better days. And, of course, if his creditors had wanted his old shoes, Jack wouldn't have been able to keep even these on his feet.

In his old life, Jack had been a star. In his new life, he was a clerk at an Eighth Avenue videotape rental store, Video Spot. More than that, he lived in a narrow apartment upstairs with the store's owner, Anne Napolitano. Not only clerk, but stud. Hey, it was a living. It was either that or the streets, where Anne had found him and from which she'd rescued him out of the kindness of her heart and an attraction she felt as soon as she laid eyes on him.

Anne Napolitano was very different from the kind of woman Jack was accustomed to. For one thing, she wasn't cool, she was fiery. He never had to persuade her or bribe her to make love; her own passion often outstripped his. Where his preference had always been for ashen-haired thin young women in their twenties with small breasts, Anne was over thirty and as dark as a gypsy, black-eyed, round-hipped, and full-bosomed. She had thick, dark curling hair as tempestuous as she was herself. Where his other lovers had worn casual loose garments of expensive washed silk, Anne wore tight-fitting inexpensive clothing that showed off her voluptuous curves.

Yet, while Anne Napolitano might not be 1990s hip, she was truly street savvy. She possessed both intelligence and a certain kind of wisdom, the common sense that comes through living, tough living.

She was totally uninhibited. When she felt like yelling, Anne yelled. When she felt like crying, she cried. When she was moved to laugh, she threw her head back, and she roared happily until her face got red. In his earlier life as a star, Jack Lucas would not have looked twice at an Anne Napolitano. She wasn't his type. As the daughter of a large, noisy Brooklyn Italian family, Anne was simply too real, too alive, too earthy for the so-called superior Jack to be comfortable with. Now, of course, he had no options. Anne had taken him in, she had fed him, sheltered him, given him a job, made frequent passionate love with him, and mothered him half to death, when she wasn't ordering him around. And there was almost nothing he could do about it.

Now she was standing in front of him, peeved, her fists on her hips, her head cocked.

"Are you going to do a little work today or not?" Anne demanded.

"Out there!" Jack's eyes rolled toward the shop, where a crowd of lunch-hour customers were pawing through the racks of tapes, looking for a movie to keep them company and make the oncoming night less lonely.

"They're not terrorists," Anne pointed out calmly. "Jack, they're just ordinary, normal people, like you and me."

And just how normal was that? Jack asked himself as he took another pull at the bourbon bottle. Who's normal? Edwin Malnick was normal, until, suddenly and without warning, he wasn't.

Anne regarded the whiskey sourly. "Breakfast of Champions, right?"

With a grunt, Jack pulled his ass unwillingly from the chair and made his way into the store. As soon as he hit the selling floor he was confronted and trapped by a fat young woman with frizzy hair and lipstick on her teeth.

"Excuse me. Can you help me, please? I'm at an absolute loss!" The woman spoke rapidly and without taking a breath. "I've been looking for an hour, I'm losing my mind! I'm sort of in the mood for a Katherine Hepburn-y, Cary Grant-y kinda thing, you know, zany? Nothing heavy, I couldn't take heavy. I'm looking for something zany. I need zany."

Jack just stared at her, her anxious babble washing over him without leaving an imprint of meaning.

"Or something modern, maybe," she went on, oblivious. "A Goldie Hawn-y, Chevy Chase-y kind of thing, y'know? I wanna laugh. I have to laugh tonight, really. Oh, oh!" exclaimed the woman, in sudden inspiration. "I know! Do you have anything with that comedian who's on that TV show? What is it . . . you know . . . yeah, *On the Radio*. You know, the guy that says, 'Hey . . . forgive me!' "

The comic catch phrase woke him out of his lethargy and made him scowl ferociously. *On the Radio* had proved to be the monster hit Jack Lucas had once hoped it would be, only now the star of the show was somebody else. Some asshole whose careless words hadn't cost eight lives.

"I get such a kick outta the way he says that . . . he's so goddamn adorable! Didn't he make a movie? That would be perfect. I need something like that, a funny no-brainy kinda thing. . . ."

Furious, Jack reached under the counter and brought out an adult X-rated video. He handed it to the customer.

"Great!" She turned the box around to read the title. *"Ordinary Peepholes?"* She threw Jack a puzzled look.

"It's a kind of big titty, spread-cheeky kind of thing," Jack explained blandly.

This was too much for Anne, who'd overheard most of it. "Excuse me," she said to the customer. "I just want to borrow him for a minute."

"You're gonna love that," Jack assured the fat woman, and Anne scowled. Grabbing him tightly by the arm, she led him back into the Video Spot office and closed the door behind them.

"That was a frightening woman." Jack shook his head. "I hate desperate people."

"Honey, sweetie, you hate people. Period. Are you in one of your moods today, baby?" Anne demanded, half-amused, half-irritated. "Is this one of those days when you're in—whaddya call it?—an emotional abyss? Talk to me, 'cause I don't understand these moods."

"Anne, they're my moods. If you want to understand moods, have one of your own!" he retorted.

Anne looked peeved, then her features softened.

"Jack, baby," she said quietly, "take the day off, all right? Why don't you go upstairs? I'll cook tonight."

"Okay," he told her grudgingly, going back with a feeling of relief to his tabloid and his bottle.

After dinner, which was lasagna, heavy on the meat sauce the way Jack liked it, they got up from the little dining area and moved over to the only slightly larger living-room area to watch *On the Radio.*

Anne laughed loudly at the sitcom, her dark eyes flashing, her black curls bobbing, her large breasts shaking with enjoyment. Jack threw her a dirty look. He hated her laughing at this show. He hated anybody laughing at this show, but especially Anne. He considered it a form of betrayal.

"Well, it's funny! Whaddya want from me?" She tried to stifle her laughter, but giggles kept escaping.

"It's not funny," Jack growled, furious. "It's sophomoric . . . and mindless . . . and dumb!"

"Then why the hell do we watch it all the time?"

The question, so simple and logical, so painful, stung Jack, and he exploded. He watched it to torture himself, what else? To dwell on what might have been, like a tongue probing into an excruciatingly rotten tooth.

The words flew out of him without punctuation or pause, bitter, envious words that cut him to speak. "Because it makes me feel good to see how not funny it is and how America doesn't know the first thing about funny, which makes it easier not being a famous funny television celebrity because that would just mean that I'm not really talented."

"Hey! For . . . give me!" The actor delivered the line that had made him a star, and the laugh track went crazy with hysterical laughter and applause. This was the moment the home viewers waited for each week, the high point of this top-ten sitcom. The catch phrase that should have made Jack Lucas a household name.

Anne stood up and walked over to Jack's chair, shaking her head in amused sympathy. "You know that you're a sick fuck? I don't know why you torture yourself." She rapped on his head. "Too many thoughts, too crowded in there. You're too self-absorbed." As Jack pushed her hand away in irritation Anne added, "You should read a book." She picked up her plump paperback novel and turned the pages to find her place.

"It's important to think," Jack retorted. "It's what separates us from lentils, and people who read books like"—he glanced contemptuously over at the cover of Anne's book—*'Love Song.'* His words came out fuzzy, slurred by drink.

"Great book. Dumb title," Anne said defensively. Jack had hurt her feelings again; he was doing that a lot more these days. What was changing between them? Jack was hiding more and more deeply in the bottle, hiding away from her, too.

"Ya know, you used to like that about me," Anne told him as Jack got up to pour more bourbon into his glass. "You used to say you liked that I didn't make you think all the time. That we could just be together and not think."

He took a deep slug of the booze and threw himself back down on the sofa in front of the television set. "Yeah, well, suicidal paranoics will say anything to get laid."

That did it. Deeply wounded, and really mad now, Anne Napolitano stood up with dignity. "Have another drink," she said bitterly. "It's on the house . . . like everything else!"

And clutching her romance novel, she stalked into the bedroom, slamming the door behind her. Jack didn't notice; he was sunk in gloom, glaring blearily at the tiny screen where some asshole was enjoying the money and fame that was supposed to have been Jack's own, the success that was snatched away before he could even catch a whiff of it. Success that would have been his if some nerd with no life of his own hadn't twisted Jack's own around so fatally. Anne was right; this was self-inflicted torture, but he couldn't pull his eyes away from the television screen or get the idiotic canned laughter out of his ears.

All he could do was drink to dull the pain, so Jack Lucas drank and drank and drank. Yet the pain, instead of dulling, grew sharper and more biting, until he couldn't endure the sitcom or this cramped apartment or his own rotten life for even another sixty seconds. . . .

"Madness!" he yelled, meaning the sitcom, his life, his relationships, and all the shit coming down in the world. He snatched up the bottle of Jack Daniels, now half-empty. Grabbing his coat off the hook on the door, he lumbered down the stairs and out into the night. The front door of the shabby building, with its doorjambs of splintered old wood, caught his favorite Versace raincoat on his way out, a large rotten sliver hooking into it and tearing the preposterously expensive fabric.

Swell. Terrific. As if he didn't look like a bum already, with his long hair uncombed and his face unshaved, a ripped raincoat added that *je ne sais quoi* that made the image complete. Jack Lucas yanked the coat free and the action threw him off balance, which was precarious enough anyway, with all the bourbon he'd been swallowing. He went flying forward, to crash against a garbage can, overturn it, and go sprawling into the garbage-strewn puddle on the wet street.

It was raining, of course. Ugly, cold, wet, pissing rain. What else was missing?

Staggering to his feet, Jack checked the bourbon

bottle to make sure it hadn't broken. Thank heaven
for tiny little mercies, it hadn't. He moved away
slowly, walking east. East, where the magic of Fifth
Avenue beckoned, even though Jack was too drunk
to know where he was going. All he knew was that
he wanted to get away from Eighth Avenue, as far
away as his stumbling boots would carry him. Thun-
der rumbled in the east, and occasional flashes of
lightning eerily lit up the sky.

In a couple of crosstown blocks the neighborhood
began to alter dramatically, from Eighth's run-down
two- and three-story buildings called "taxpayers"—
because all they did was take up room and pay the
property taxes—to the gleaming steel-and-glass cor-
porate monoliths of Avenue of the Americas to the
pricey real estate of Fifth. Angry and hurting, Jack
Lucas could glimpse his old apartment building
through the haze of raindrops; lights were on in almost every apartment behind the steel-and-concrete
terraces, and the entire building shone like a star.
And it was about as far removed from his reach as
a star, too. He'd need a spaceship to get back to it.
The sight of his old pad depressed Jack unutterably;
even looking at it from across the street made him
realize just how far from it he'd come, and exactly
how low he'd sunk. He was so low, he had to look
up to look down.

Jack turned away, heading north, and a few minutes later he found himself across the street from the
Plaza Hotel, that classic landmark of the good life.
The Plaza, built in the style of a French château on
the southern fringes of Central Park, cleverly designed to appear as though the verdant stretches of
the park were its own private game preserve.

He knew the Plaza well. Jack was too drunk to
really focus, but vague wisps crossed his memory,
dim but tantalizing recollections of power lunches in
the hotel's elegant Edwardian Room, leisurely and

expensive dinners in the Oak Room, succulent oysters washed down with Muscadet or imported beer at the Oyster Bar, potent rum drinks and barbecued munchies at Trader Vic's. Yeah, the Plaza. *His* Plaza. Jack's shambling feet carried him slowly across the street to where the patient horses stood hitched to their fancy ribbon-decked carriages, waiting in the rain with downcast heads to trot leisured people with money around Central Park.

As Jack crossed Fifty-eighth Street, the hotel's revolving door turned and disgorged a handsome man in his early forties, wearing a neat Burberry raincoat and carrying a crocodile briefcase. Behind him came a bellman with the luggage, and with him was his son, a diminutive carbon copy about seven years old, whose clothing was as expensive as his old man's, and whose demeanor was exactly as sober. In his hands the boy was carrying a painted wooden Pinocchio doll with pointed hat, long nose, and staring eyes. The doll had been acquired at the expensive FAO Schwartz toy store across Fifth Avenue as a souvenir of this trip.

They headed for a taxi stand, which usually held a dozen or more cabs, waiting at the curb for fares from the Plaza. But tonight, with the rain, the cab rank was empty, and a cab would be hard to come by in midtown Manhattan. The man began to wave his briefcase wildly, trying to hail an empty taxi.

"Hey, buddy? Help a guy out?"

The moment the pair, father and son, reached the curbside, a homeless panhandler accosted them, begging for a handout. The man shook his head brusquely and turned away.

"Help me out with a quarter," the bum insisted. "C'mon."

"Get away from me," the man demanded, and the bum, yelling obscenities, reached out and grabbed hold of the Burberry with his filthy hand.

The personal contact drove the wealthy man into a frenzy. How dare a greasy bum lay a hand on him! Striking out wildly with his briefcase, he caught the panhandler on the temple, but before he could do more damage, the Plaza doorman intervened, driving the bum away and escorting the man into an empty cab his doorman's whistle had summoned.

Jack Lucas stood paralyzed, unable to tear his eyes away from the scene. He didn't see the little boy approaching him until a voice very close to him spoke.

"Mr. Bum?"

Jack looked down. The privileged child stood regarding him gravely for a minute, then he held out the Pinocchio doll. For a moment Jack was confused; what did the kid want?

"Grayson," called his father's voice from inside the taxi. "Grayson, come here at once."

The child thrust the doll into Jack's surprised arms and trotted back across the street obediently. He climbed into the backseat and the taxicab pulled away from the curb with a grinding of gears and disappeared around the corner, heading south on Fifth.

Jack stared after the car until it was out of sight. Then he looked down at the doll in his hands. It stared back at him with wide painted eyes, and its long nose was like some accusing finger. Pinocchio, shit. You know, he almost kind of liked the damn thing. He tucked it under his arm and set off in search of Jiminy Cricket.

It stopped raining, and the homeless were settling down on the wet pavement to fall asleep the best way they could. Some were wrapped in newspapers as a feeble attempt to keep away the cold. Others were better provided for. The lucky ones, or the smarter ones—take your pick—had created beds out of flattened cardboard boxes, and were lying on them in-

stead of on the concrete. For the first time Jack really
saw them, this hopeless band of outcast men and
women with no roof over their heads. For two years
he had lived virtually in the shadow of these people,
but had never really seen them before. Even in his
drunken state, they made him shudder as he realized
how close, how precariously close to them he himself was.

The equestrian statue of Victory leading the horse
of General William Tecumseh ("War is hell") Sherman had been recently regilded at enormous public
expense. Even in darkness it shone now like a lit
beacon made of solid gold. The Union general who
had destroyed Atlanta and burned a mile-wide swath
through Georgia from Atlanta to the sea sat boldly
on his horse, while the goddess of Victory, Nike,
held the laurel wreath of the conquerer high. But that
war ended more than a century ago; nobody really
cared about Sherman except the pigeons, the Japanese tourists with their cameras, and the footsore
who sank gratefully down on the base of the statue
to rest.

Jack Lucas slumped down below the statue and
leaned his back against the cold marble of the plinth.
Taking a long swig from his nearly empty bottle, he
set Pinocchio on his knee and regarded him with
solemn melancholy.

"You ever read any Nietzsche?" he asked the doll,
who didn't answer.

"Nietzsche says that there are two kinds of people
in the world. People who are destined for greatness,
like . . . Walt Disney . . . and . . . Hitler . . . and
then there's the rest of us. He called us the Bungled
and the Botched. We get teased. We sometimes get
close to greatness, but we never get there. We're the
expendable masses. We get pushed in front of trains,
take poisoned aspirins, get gunned down in Dairy

Queens.'' He took another drink, almost draining the bottle.

''You wanna hear my new title for my biography, my little Italian friend?'' Pinocchio looked back, and Jack perceived a yes in that painted wooden smile. *It Was No Fucking Picnic: the Jack Lucas Story.* Like it? Just nod yes or no.'' He tilted the doll's head up and down to say yes. *''Il Nouva Está Fuckin' Picnicko,''* he essayed in a kind of bastard mock Italian to make the wooden doll understand better. Did it work? Jack thought so.

''You're a good kid,'' he told Pinocchio almost fondly. ''Just say no to drugs. . . .'' Raising the bottle, Jack took one more drink. Depressed as he was, that last drink pushed him over the edge from melancholy into desolation. He saw himself now as lost, a stranger to the world, completely cut off and shut out from the rest of humanity, and in his drunken state he knew it with remarkable clarity.

''You ever get the feeling sometimes that you're being punished for your sins?'' Jack asked the silent doll. Punished for my sins, he thought. As though there was enough punishment in this world to pay off what I did . . .

Four

Jack felt calm, bathed in a peace that was almost beautiful. There's nothing like making a decision to give a man's mind a rest. It was such a simple decision, really, he thought as he fastened the heavy-cement block around his right ankle. Such a commonsense answer to all his problems; why hadn't he thought of it before? He wound strips of his trousers around the second block and attached it to his left ankle, tucking dear little Pinocchio inside. At least he wouldn't go alone. He had a friend now, a friend who might be a little short on facial expression and vocabulary, but one who didn't judge him, who didn't argue, who always had a cheerful smile for Jack Lucas. They'd go together.

Jack stood up and moved his feet. Great; the blocks were heavy enough so that, no matter how he might struggle to swim, they would do their job and pull him down to the bottom of the filthy, oily river. The East River. Jack Lucas still had class, no matter what. When he took himself out, he'd go in style, on the snobbish east side, where he belonged. No measly Hudson River for a star.

Somebody once said that to the rational mind, life is a race between natural death and suicide. Jack Lucas was just about to lose that race.

There were a few drops left in the Jack Daniel's bottle, and Jack tilted his head back and drained them. Jack and Jack. The lyric from his program's theme song kept turning around in his head . . . *Hit the road, Jack*. . . . How appropriate, how fitting. He didn't intend to come back no more. He flung the empty bottle away and smiled to hear it shatter on the concrete pavement. Another ending.

In the cold moonlight, under the promenade, the river looked serene and inviting, even beckoning. Here is surcease, it said. Here is rest for the weary. O, come all you faithless. . . . Jack took a step forward, mesmerized by the light reflecting from its surface. It was time to go. He took another step.

There was a harsh grinding of gears and the squealing of heavy tires; car doors slammed, and the sound of ugly laughter broke the promenade's silence. But thanks to his drunken oblivion and his fuzzy focus on suicide, Jack didn't hear any of it.

"What's going on?" demanded a rough voice behind him, and this time Jack turned, only to be blinded by bright white headlights. Lured by the promise of the river, he hadn't noticed the 4×4 that was now parked about ten yards away. Two men got out and started toward him. As his eyes became accustomed to the glare of the headlights Jack could see that they weren't men at all, but boys. Maybe eighteen, nineteen. Maybe only seventeen. One of them wore a leather jacket and carried a baseball bat in his right hand. The other wore a windbreaker.

Both of them were carrying cans of gasoline.

Jack was shit-faced, but not too drunk to comprehend the significance of the gas cans. A chill of fear ran through his veins and he began to sweat ice water.

"I said, what's going on?" the boy in the leather jacket demanded, this time in a louder voice as he came up close to Jack. "What are you doing here, man?" His face was menacing, his eyes hooded and angry.

This was going to be bad; Jack knew it instinctively, but his brain was too befuddled from drink for him to react quickly. Even if he were sober, with the heavy cement blocks attached to his legs, he wouldn't be able to run. Before he could answer, the boy in the leather jacket got him in the gut with the bat, hard, knocking the wind out of him and making him sink to his knees, retching and gasping hoarsely to catch his breath. The other boy set the gasoline cans down and began to unscrew them.

Jack Lucas had read about cases like this, where juvenile delinquents set bums on fire, usually sleeping bums. The boys almost never got caught, but the bums died. Every year at least thirty homeless men died that hideous way in New York, screaming in agony as the flames devoured the flesh from their bones. Now it was going to be his turn. Instead of sinking quietly into the cool embrace of the peaceful water, Jack's death would be literally hell on earth, the fire this time. Punishment for his sins, and with a vengeance. No, he didn't want this, not this kind of death. It was too big a price to pay. Between the terrible fear and the harsh pain from the blow to his belly, Jack's mind was shocked into a state approaching sobriety. His body, though, out of condition, limbs paralyzed by alcohol, continued to betray him.

"You shouldn't hang around this neighborhood," growled the boy in the leather jacket, with a grin of malice. He kicked Jack in the side, just to drive his point home, and because he enjoyed it.

"I . . . I was just leaving," Jack gasped, his arms wound tightly around his body, protecting his belly. His eye never left the lethal cans of gasoline.

"People spend a lot of hard-earned money for this neighborhood," the tough continued, prodding Jack with the end of the bat. "It's not fair, looking out their windows to see your ass asleep on the streets."

"Yes . . . I . . . I agree."

"That's good. That's very good." The hoodlum in the leather jacket grinned and turned to his friend. "You believe this drunk?" The delinquent wearing the windbreaker shook his head no. "Me, neither. Man, get the fuckin' gas." He grabbed Jack by the hair, to keep him from getting away.

Windbreaker handed Leather Jacket the gas can; Leather Jacket lifted it high over his head. The twisted malicious grin never left his face as Leather Jacket allowed a thin stream of the flammable fuel to dribble over Jack's clothing. This was the good part; the fun was just getting started.

"No . . . no, *please,*" Jack whimpered. He didn't want to die this way. In fact, now that he was pretty close to sober, he didn't want to die at all. But certainly not as a shrieking human torch.

The boys were laughing now, and Jack Lucas's body was drenched in gasoline. It was hopeless; he couldn't fight, and even if he could, there was no way he could take them both on. It was the end for him and Pinocchio. Leather Jacket had him tightly by the hair, pulling his head back. Jack closed his eyes while regrets of every kind crowded into his brain, too late.

"Hold, varlet, or feel the sting of my shaft! Unhand that errant knight in the name of Blanche des Fleurs!"

The voice came ringing out of the darkness, strong, deep, clear, and dramatic. The adolescent hoodlums turned in surprise, their eyes searching the shadows. Even Jack opened his eyes, startled.

"What the fu . . . ? Ugggghh!" An arrow came whistling through the air and slammed hard into Windbreaker's groin. It was an arrow with a rubber suction tip, from a child's archery set, but even so it hurt like hell.

Leather Jacket dropped Jack's head with a snarl, ready to rumble. Jack peered into the shadows and a small figure took a step forward. My God, it was someone out of an heroic epic of the Middle Ages! Robin Hood or somebody. Was he dreaming? He saw a long cloak, a hat with a feather, a bow over the shoulder, a quiver of arrows. He had to be dreaming! He must have jumped in after all. This whole episode, even the teenage hoodlums, had to be one last hallucination of a drowning man, sinking to the bottom of the East River with bricks strapped to his legs.

Then the figure took another step forward; now he could be seen much more clearly in the light of the street lamp. The cloak was not a cloak but a filthy, ragged army blanket pinned clumsily at the shoulder, the rakish cap, a woman's discarded sequined beret into which twigs and leaves had been somehow fastened. This was no medieval hero, but an ordinary, common tramp. Only crazier, a lot crazier.

Yet Jack could see that there was nothing common or ordinary about the small man's face. It shone with a calm intelligence and twinkled with humor. The eyes were wide and innocent, the nose long and straight, the mouth smiling, and the chin covered by a dark beard. There was no fear in this face, and no menace, but no mistaking it, there was real insanity there. The man appeared to be fairly young, not more than thirty-five, despite the maturity of his beard.

"It's just a bum," Leather Jacket snarled. He brandished the gas can. "You know, there's enough in here for the two of you."

The small man did not appear fazed by the threat. "You speak English?" he roared. "Let the bum go, dipshit! Mendacity! Why are two attractive city squires like you abusing a knight like this?"

Leather Jacket's lip curled in disgust. "You a faggot?"

"Faggot?" The stranger seemed surprised by the word, and considered it with seriousness. "No, but I do believe in faeries. I advise you to let him go," he added quietly.

"You advise us!" A harsh laughter escaped Leather Jacket's lips. This dumb faggot was gonna get it. Both these bums were gonna get it.

The stranger chuckled. "You're outnumbered, son." He waved his hand.

Other figures slowly materialized out of the shadows behind him. They were homeless vagrants, three of them, each one perhaps harmless, even pathetic, but put them together in the dark and the sight of them was something unnerving. One of them was mumbling to himself, obviously a psychotic. Actually, they were probably all crazy as bedbugs, especially their shabby Robin Hood of a leader. This was very creepy. Even Jack was afraid of them, and the two adolescents kept shifting their gaze to make certain they weren't surrounded.

"It's the fuckin' Night of the Living Dead," whispered one, not without fear. Weapons seemed definitely called for. Both delinquents pulled out their switchblades and snapped them open. Windbreaker appeared nervous; he didn't like what was starting to happen here. This was supposed to be more predictable; it wasn't like it was the first time they'd pulled this stunt. But Leather Jacket made an effort to maintain his macho bravado.

Jack Lucas only stared, mystified and a little alarmed. What was going down here? The delinquents might be homicidal, but at least they weren't irrational. On the other hand, his rescuer definitely appeared to be delusional, possibly psychotic, and maybe even murderous. Was Jack about to go from the fire to the frying pan?

"C'mon," Leather Jacket urged his companion.

"Go for it! What the hell are they gonna do? They can't do nothin'."

"Nothing! They can do nothing!" The stranger cried out in pained exasperation at the abysmal grammar. *"Gentlemen!"* He took a step or two backward into the shadows and raised his hand. It was a signal to his little band.

Immediately, and stupefyingly, the bums burst into song, caroling about New York in June and a Gershwin tune. They were a country mile away from the tune, some of the lyrics were wrong, and one of them was totally out of sync, yet the ragtag little chorus put real heart into the old standard. It was the single most surreal moment of Jack Lucas's life.

"Shit!" Leather Jacket spat, infuriated. He had some dim comprehension that his masculinity was being mocked here, and it was time to kick some ass. He brandished the knife, ready to use it. The bums' leader smiled genially, and his face lit up like a kid's at Christmas.

"Oh, look, it's showtime." He beamed. "Y'know, boys," he continued in a benign, almost fatherly voice, taking off the sequined cap he was wearing, reaching into it and pulling out a long sock with a round bulge in the toe. As he continued speaking he twirled the sock high over his head until it formed a perfect circle like a gaucho's bolo, achieving momentum until it was only a kind of circular blur.

"There are only three things in the world you need . . . respect for all kinds of life, a good bowel movement on a regular basis, and a nice navy blazer. Oh, and one more thing! Never . . . take . . . your . . . eyes . . . off . . . the . . . ball!" With the last word and a snap of his wrist, he let the sock fly with deadly accuracy.

The sock whizzed through the air, catching Leather Jacket square between the eyes with the tennis ball that was tucked into the toe. The boy groaned in pained shock and, dropping his switch-blade knife, rubbed at the lump on his head. The merry band's leader smiled with simple pleasure and reached for another sock.

"Of course," he remarked conversationally, start-ing to twirl his second weapon, "the ability to bean a shithead can be a fabulous advantage." He ap-peared to be enjoying himself immensely.

Windbreaker had already seen one graphic exam-ple of the murderous effectiveness of the crazy's homemade weapon. He didn't need to see another, especially since he appeared to be the target of this one. With a yell, he took to his heels, darting past the bums into the 4×4. With a grinding of gears, he peeled rubber, leaving his friend behind in the hands of God only knew what.

The leader strode swiftly over to Jack, who was huddled on the cold concrete. He bent to retrieve the delinquent's knife and asked Jack with gentle con-cern, "Are you all right?"

Jack Lucas flinched as though he'd been struck and shrank away from the bum's touch. He was com-pletely disoriented, overcome by the alcohol, the swift turn of events, his fear, and the nauseating reek of the gasoline that covered him head to foot. "Please don't hurt me," he begged.

"Why?" asked Robin Hood, sounding suddenly perfectly sane. "So you can be healthy when you jump? Nah!"

Next to him, the boy in the leather jacket was still groaning and clutching at his head. Working quickly, the leader pulled a rope out from under his tattered blanket cloak and tied Leather Jacket's hands behind him, making neat unbreakable knots. Then he stood and helped Jack gently to his feet. He handed the knife to Jack, who took it with a shudder of revulsion and hurled it away, into the river. Taking Jack's elbow, he began to lead him away.

"You can't leave me tied up out here alone, you fucking faggot!" screamed the boy, panic diluting the anger in his voice. He struggled with his bonds, but the rope held good and tight. The delinquent in the leather jacket had been tied in a deliberately awkward position, kneeling on the sidewalk, his butt up in the air.

"You're not going to be alone. Come and geeeet it," called the stranger invitingly, and two of the bums began to shuffle forward. The boy moaned in fear.

Jack found it hard to stand, let alone walk. His gut was on fire from the blow with the bat, and every muscle in his neck and shoulders ached with tension. "I need a drink," he muttered, more to himself than to his rescuer.

"Hey, I know a fabulous place with great ambience." The small man beamed. Kneeling down, he unfasted the cement blocks from Jack's legs and placed the Pinocchio doll into Jack's arms with an almost graceful tenderness. Once again, he took Jack by the arm, steering him along.

All Jack Lucas wanted now was to see his home, a bathtub, a bottle, and Anne. The last thing in the world he wanted was to go along with this loony derelict who suffered from the delusion that he was some kind of white knight. But, somehow, he didn't seem to have a choice. Reluctantly, still trying to figure out the dizzying events of the past ten minutes, Jack stumbled along behind his savior.

Five

For most of his life Jack had heard and used the phrase "the dregs of humanity" without once giving much thought or understanding to it. Now, unexpectedly, he was right in the middle of them. Real-life low-down dregs, the human sludge left in the bottom of the barrel when the good stuff was all used up. It was not a pretty sight. It was a scene out of Gorky, or worse, Dante. *The Lower Depths* maybe, or one of the waiting rooms of hell. Even drunk, Jack Lucas recognized that these people had not only touched bottom, bottom had become their zip code. Here before his eyes, in the unsavory flesh, was the living personification of Nietzsche's Bungled and Botched.

The forgotten, the nameless, the homeless, the hopeless, the mentally ill, the alkies, the druggies, a ragtag army beyond redemption, people who had long forgotten the ordinary daily commerce of the world, were gathered here, in the litter-strewn area underneath the steel stanchions of the Manhattan Bridge. Above their heads, the bridge's heavy suspension cables sang an eerie wind song while swaying in the gusts of the evening. Below, a cluster of men—mostly men, with one or two women so tattered and filthy that their gender was unrecognizable—sat around on the ground like a defeated army, their generals dead, their troops decimated, their host scattered, their eagles lost, seized by the Goths.

Many of these people owned nothing apart from the threadbare clothing on their backs. Others, equally if not more pathetic, had collected paltry, useless bits and pieces, culled from what the real world had cast aside. These treasures they kept always close by them, tied up in garbage bags on which they slept, or piled high into rickety shopping carts lifted from the local supermarkets, over which they stood a weary, endless watch.

Some of them owned mongrel dogs, who scavenged from fire to fire, begging for crusts. There were even two or three cats who called this place home, exchanging their affection for human warmth. The cats kept a large part of the vermin population at bay.

Athough it was a motley and unrelated assemblage, Jack realized that most of its members had something besides homelessness in common—alcohol. They drank whatever they could get their hands on, mostly pint bottles of cheap fortified sweet wine, which they bought in Korean liquor shops with the dimes and nickels they cadged during the day. By now, almost all of them were drunk or well on their way to being drunk. In this, Jack Lucas found himself their blood brother. If he'd been sober, it might have made him think. Yet he still felt superior to this human refuse; he had class, he had education, and most of all, he had somewhere he could go.

This was the downtime, the night hours when these homeless could gather together here on their turf, light a few fires in garbage cans to provide some semblance of warmth. Here they could drink, argue, reminisce, trade lies, weep, and watch the city rats, some of them bigger than house cats, go scurrying by on their unspeakable night errands.

Grinning cheerfully, Jack's new pal, his cicerone, his personal Virgil, led him right into the heart of this urban jungle and sat him down against the bridge's pillar so that he could socialize and make friends. The river's rankness rose on the night air and assaulted Jack's nostrils. On the East River, the night traffic went by. Old freighters of dubious registry, tugboats, and garbage scows, paddling through the scummy waters. Above them, on the FDR Drive, Mercedes and BMWs headed north to Sutton Place.

For the bearded man, this gathering under the bridge was a gala social occasion, the celebration of his triumph against the juvenile delinquents. For Jack, it was a nightmare from which he struggled in vain to wake up.

What the hell was he doing here, in the middle of the night, with a dull ache in his gut, stinking of gasoline and bourbon, listening to the garbage boats chugging by on the river and to this bunch of board-certified crazies raving on, arguing about the profundities of life? He had to be as nutty as they were. Jack sat as far away from them as possible and tried to tune out, just like his Pinocchio doll, but their loud lunatic words kept drifting into his unwilling consciousness.

"There ain't no justice in life," the large black man in the old Vietnam combat jacket was growling. "There's just satisfaction. And the death penalty's just another violation of my constitutional right to satisfaction, goddamn it!"

The long-haired pimply kid, who looked like a refugee from the flower-child 1960s, leaned forward to make his point. "So you mean, if somebody like killed your mother, you wouldn't want him dead?"

"Sure I would!" The black man's brow furrowed indignantly. "But *I* should get to kill him, goddamn it!"

The Irishman agreed. He nodded his head vigorously, and the ash from his burning cigarette dropped all over his ancient filthy overcoat. "He gets to kill him," he explained earnestly to the hippie. "That's democracy, see?"

Jack Lucas shook his head. "This is it," he mumbled to himself. "I'm in hell. Damned to an eternity of idiotic conversation."

"Great place, huh?" His guide, the perfect host, the poor man's Robin Hood, beamed cheerily at him. He appeared to be genuinely happy here, and at home. He seemed to know everybody, and everybody knew him. Repelled, Jack turned away without reply.

A bloodcurdling scream ripped the air. Jack jumped in his skin and looked around. It was the Irishman, caught up suddenly in the whirlpool of his madness, being sucked into the vortex and screaming his lungs out in horror. God alone could guess what his hallucination might be. Then a second scream rang out. Robin Hood joined him, just to keep him company, and the two men howled together like a pair of starving coyotes.

Then, as suddenly as they'd started, they stopped screaming. "How are you tonight?" the Irishman asked pleasantly, as though nothing out of the ordinary had happened here. The nameless terrors of five seconds ago were history now, forgotten.

"Not bad, John, and you?" Robin Hood's eyes crinkled happily from the warmth of his smile.

"Can't complain." The Irishman took a long drag on his cigarette and flicked off the live ash. It flew through the air and landed on Jack Lucas's gas-soaked sleeve. Immediately, the gas ignited and burst into flame.

"Oh, fuck!" Jack scrambled clumsily to his feet, his face a distorted mask of fear. His raincoat sleeve was on fire, burning merrily, and Jack tore at it, dancing frantically around, yelling and fumbling until he managed to get it off his body and hurl it to the ground. After he stomped the blaze out, he checked for damage. The fire had scorched his hand, which began to throb very painfully.

It was a spectacular break in the evening's activities. Jack had just put on a show for them, and the bums, appreciative, broke into enthusiastic applause. There were cheers and whistles. Only the black man grumbled, because he'd been holding center stage, and Jack's crazy antics had taken the group's attention away from him. "Crazy fuck," he muttered.

"So what do you think of the death penalty?" the hippie kid asked the Irishman. Show was over, and everything was back to normal. Unless Jack Lucas burst into flame again, he was no longer interesting to them.

"Death's definitely a penalty. It ain't no fuckin' gift. Life's too goddamn short."

Their words blurred in Jack's ears. He was really starting to crash now. Fatigue was numbing him and he was a very long way from home. Gathering up his sodden raincoat, he started to take his leave of the little gathering. "I better be going. . . ."

But the Irishman wasn't about to let him get away so easily. "Have a drink." He pushed his bottle into Jack's face, and when Jack waved it away, he roared, "Have a drink, damn it!"

Remembering the screaming, Jack thought it best not to argue the point. Accepting the dirty bottle, he took a pull. The fiery liquor, cheap and rough and totally unlike the smooth expensive bourbon Jack was accustomed to, scorched a painful path down his throat and into his belly. He bent over, hacking, coughing, trying to breathe.

"I think they like you," his new friend said shyly, and raised his hand. At once, as if it was a signal, his little band of bums broke into "that song about liking June in New York" Totally inappropriate and completely out of left field, but they seemed to enjoy it.

By now, the fumes of the cheap booze had risen to Jack's brain, making him dizzy. He had the sudden sinking realization that he was about to pass out, here, under an abutment of the Manhattan Bridge with only the terminally weird for company. As he blacked out, the last thing he remembered hearing was the hippie yelling enthusiastically, "You were phenomenal tonight, Parry. Fuckin' Super-Bum!"

Super-Bum? Jack wondered drowsily, and then the darkness came down and closed everything off.

Six

It was the sound, the drip-drip-dripping of the water, one slow agonizing drop at a time, that made Jack Lucas finally open his eyes. He turned his head to see where the water was coming from. Big mistake. He should not have tried to move. The headache from hell grabbed his eye sockets and the base of his skull and twisted, hard. Nausea made a lump of burning bile rise in his throat, and he shuddered, falling back on the bed. Shit, was he hung over!

Where the hell was he? Bed. He was in bed. Or rather, *on* bed. Only it wasn't exactly a bed, in that it didn't have pillows, or sheets, or even a box spring. Jack was lying on a mattress on the floor. Except for his beloved boots, he was still fully clothed. Floor? What floor? Gingerly, he lifted his head up again, and the hangover kicked in, but he opened only one eye and gradually his vision cleared.

He was in a basement somewhere. Pipes ran overhead; he could hear them banging and gurgling, and one of them was obviously doing the dripping. The floor was concrete. A boiler stood nearby, making the room almost intolerably warm. Every few seconds live steam puffed out of it. Right; he was in the boiler room of a basement. A boiler room, yet it was furnished . . . in a very strange way. Where the hell was he and how the hell did he get here?

"Hi! Welcome back! How are you feeling?" A

cheerful voice, bright blue eyes, a cherubic bearded face, a big dopey smile, and slowly it all came back.

Last night. The narrow escape from those hoodlums with the gas cans. The river. He'd tried to drown himself, but he'd been attacked. His belly still ached horribly from the baseball-bat attack; it must be deeply bruised. He flashed on his companion, with his raggedy cloak and his homemade weapons. This mental case and his merry band of schizos had saved his life. Vaguely he remembered the later scene under the Manhattan Bridge, and Jack realized that he must have passed out there. But why had he been dragged here? What did this lunatic want from him?

"Have I died?" Jack muttered, squinting through his one good eye, the other closed to keep the killer headache at bay. He'd assassinate for a cigarette, even though his mouth tasted like the prop wash of a circus parade.

The small man's eyes crinkled up merrily, and he let out a roar of laughter. "Oh, no, no, nononono . . . not yet."

The laughter penetrated Jack's hangover like an alarm siren, and the headache escalated to new heights of agony. "If you're going to murder me, fine. Just don't laugh." Shifting his weight on the mattress, Jack decided to try to move. It wasn't happening.

"No, no, sorry. Easy, easy," the bearded man soothed him, taking Jack around the shoulders. "Wanna get up? There you go." With surprising strength, he eased Jack up into a sitting position. "Take it real slow, now. Take a few breaths. Good, that's good."

Jack was surprised to discover that he actually felt a little better sitting up. He swung his legs over the side of the mattress, and his feet touched the concrete. Oh, wonderful. No boots. His precious Tony

Lamas with the real silver toe caps were nowhere to be seen. They'd been ripped off, either by those winos under the Manhattan Bridge or by this friendly, smiling fruitcake.

Making a huge effort, Jack stood up. He felt a little wobbly, but his legs still worked. Slowly, he looked around at the small living space the man had created here in this basement boiler room. He opened both his eyes to see better. Talk about weird!

The place was a mess, dirty and disordered. Garbage and stale food were everywhere, and some of it had rotted beyond color and smell to become something unidentifiable. There was an incredible accumulation of rubbish and trash, obviously collected from the street. In addition to the mattress on the floor, there were a couple of wobbly kitchen chairs and a rickety table with its shorty leg propped up by books. These must also have been rescued from the street before the garbage trucks got there. At the center of this rubbish, propped up against a wall, sat Pinocchio, with his unblinking eyes and his painted-on wooden smile. The only illumination in the room came from a bare bulb hanging from a string, which was probably just as well. Strong light might have destroyed the ambience, the romance of the surroundings.

This seemed to Jack to be the flopping place of a homeless bum, but with three important differences. The first thing was that there were books everywhere, hundreds of them, hardcovers and paperbacks, books that appeared to have been read and reread. The second thing was that the walls were decorated as no bum had decorated a wall before. Jack stared at the walls in astonishment.

On one wall were taped pictures taken from books and magazines and art postcards. They were all medieval in theme—knights, castles, ladies fair, scenes of jousting and chivalry; some Jack recognized as well-known illustrations and famous paintings. What they had in common was a beauty and a serenity and an evocation of a time and place dead for five hundred years, a world no one had experienced except in books in half a millennium.

On the opposite wall was a huge poster of a knight in full armor, helmed, corseleted, greaved, bucklered, shielded, and weaponed cap-a-pie, riding straight at the viewer on an armored and caparisoned war-horse. As though the warrior knight himself were not ferocious enough, someone had taken a red Magic Marker and slashed great crimson streaks over the knight and his horse, streaks that looked exactly like hellish tongues of flame. The effect was menacing, nightmarish, totally surreal. Unconsciously intimidated, Jack took a backward step, away from the picture.

He looked around him again, noticing for the first time that some of the rubbish in the room possessed a definite medieval character. A few hubcaps were fashioned into small shields on straps of old rope, and painted with strange devices. The chrome detail from an old Ford Fairlane appeared to be some kind of crudely fashioned weapon. Even the odd rags of clothing strewn about could be seen to bear the aspect of apparel from the Middle Ages. And then there was the alcove.

The third big difference between this basement hovel and an ordinary bum's room was set apart in a small alcove. In contrast to the mess in the rest of the place, the alcove was pristine, even beautiful. Many candles were lit, as though dedicated on an altar. And there *was* an altar of sorts, although the objects being venerated were bizarre indeed. Among them Jack recognized a Chinese-food takeout carton and a pair of chopsticks, a popular junky romance novel of the kind that women read, some imitation jewels, and the picture of a beautiful, virginal maiden with flowers in her long flowing golden hair. It was a print of a very famous Botticelli painting, one of the treasures of the fifteenth century. This was obviously some kind of shrine, but to what kind of deity Jack Lucas didn't know and didn't want to know. The whole business struck him as really creepy.

"Where am I?" he asked in a low voice. This goddamn place was spooking him.

"My domicile, my humble abode, my neck of the woods," answered the bearded man cheerfully, perched on one of the kitchen chairs. "Want something to eat? Because your stomach must be a real tabula rasa after last night." He threw the Latin term off easily, without stopping for breath. "How about a fruit pie?" From somewhere, the man produced something greenish and sticky in his grimy hands and shoved it under Jack Lucas's nauseated nose.

Jack recoiled instinctively. "No, thanks . . . hey, listen—"

"You're right about that one." The fellow chucked the little pie across the room. "I was off by about a couple of months. It's nice to have company," he added, rather shyly.

"Uh, where are my shoes?"

"They're—" The man broke off and leaped suddenly off the chair, his attention focusing on the overhead pipes. "What?" he yelled. "I've got company!"

Startled, Jack looked up but could see nothing. "Where . . . ?"

"What?" The man was yelling at somebody, but nobody was there.

"What?" echoed Jack, really unnerved now. The guy was talking to the air, and from the looks of it the air was answering back.

"I knew it! I knew it last night! I did, too! He's the one!"

The one? The one what?

The small man came up close to Jack and whispered loudly, ''Can you keep a secret?''

Backing off, Jack shook his head no.

''Good, because do you know what the Little People told me?''

''The Little People?'' Jack echoed nervously, humoring the madman until he could make his escape.

''They said you're the One.''

''The one what?''

The bearded man whirled and yelled up at the ceiling, ''Shut up! Get away from here!'' He darted to a shelf and grabbed up a can of air freshener. ''This will get them out of here!'' He began to spray the room with broad, sweeping strokes of the can. The chemically fake wintergreen smell and the choking spray brought on a wave of fresh nausea in Jack. Unable to breathe, he began to cough.

''Oh, God! I've got a right to say something!'' the man was shrieking now, sounding desperate. ''Leave him alone! I mean, you're tying my hands here!'' He sprayed again, gassing his hallucination. ''I'm sorry about this,'' he apologized to Jack. ''They say you're not ready to know yet.''

''I'm not,'' Jack agreed, itching to get out of there this minute. ''My shoes—''

''He is, too!'' yelled the crazy man, with another sweeping spritz of the air freshener. ''Fuck off, now! Beat it! Oh, yeah? Fly up there! Yeah . . .''

Desperate to escape from the deadly miasma of wintergreen, Jack backed into the alcove shrine.

''Heyyyy! You can't be in there!'' The note of panic in the other man's voice brought him out of there quickly.

''You're frightening him!'' the crazy accused the air. Jack backed away until his back was almost against the red-hot boiler, but the small man pursued him, kneeling down close by and peering into his face.

"Do you know who I am?"

Jack saw that the bearded man was regarding him with an earnest attention tinged with anxiety. Better play along.

"Uh . . . I'm drawing a blank." Gotta get out of here, he thought. Where the fuck are my boots?

"Well, take a guess. *Let him guess!*" he roared at thin air, reaching for the can of air spray again.

Anything but that. "Uh . . . gee . . . well . . . you seem to be some kind of vigilante."

"No, no." The bearded man shook his head vigorously. "I mean, of course, that happened along the way, but no." He leaned closer, and Jack found himself looking into a pair of bright blue eyes that sparkled with delusion. "No, I'm a knight on a very special quest."

"A quest?" echoed Jack.

"Take a look at this!" Grabbing something up, the little man thrust it proudly under Jack's nose. "What's this?"

Jack looked. "A hood ornament?"

"No, it's a sword. For the quest. But I need help, and that's why *they* sent you."

They? Oh, right. "The Little—"

"Yes. The Little People. They work for Him. So do I."

"Him?" Jack asked, certain that he didn't really want to know.

The small man leaned even closer to whisper. "God. I'm the janitor of God." Seeing Jack's horrified face, he added hastily, "Hey, I know how you feel. Hard to believe, right? Well, just listen. . . ."

Settling himself into one of the rickety kitchen chairs, he explained while Jack listened reluctantly, calculating the distance between the small man and the door, wondering if he could make it to the street without shoes.

"*They* came to *me* about a year ago. I was sitting on the john having one of those really satisfying bowel movements . . . you know the ones, that border on the mystical." And here, he screwed up his face to illustrate, straining, straining, then uttering a long, blissful sigh of release while his face looked positively beatific. "And there they were, just floating around. Hundreds of the cutest little fat people. And then they spoke. They said I had been chosen to get back something special that He had lost. But my part might be very dangerous. I said, 'Hold it right there!' You start seeing floating little fat people that tell you you're on a mission for God, that'll slap you with some really heavy thoughts. I said, 'Give me a sign.' Then *they* said, 'Look at *Progressive Architecture,* Feb. eighty-eight . . . page thirty-three.' That's pretty specific."

Leaping eagerly from his chair, the small man raced over to a pile of magazines and riffled through them, finding one and bringing it over to Jack. He leafed through the pages to find the right one, then shoved it under Jack's nose. "And there it was, plain as day!" he finished triumphantly.

Jack Lucas was locked in here with a man who heard voices and saw visions on the crapper, yet somehow he'd been sucked into the guy's story, nutty as it was. Despite himself, Jack looked at the glossy magazine. The caption running across a double-page spread read: *Real Estate Billionaire Langdon Carmichael's Tower of Power.* It was a five-page feature story, complete with color photos, about how Carmichael had acquired a nineteenth-century armory on Fifth Avenue and had spent ten million big ones fixing it up as a fortified mansion to live in.

"Langdon Carmichael?" Jack looked at the other man, puzzled.

"No, no. Right there. See it?" With a grimy finger, the bum pointed. On the page was a photo of the tycoon in his newly furnished library. Carmichael was standing proudly in front of a bookcase holding first editions and other precious objects. One of the objects, a silver goblet, had been circled heavily in black crayon.

"It's the Grail. The Holy Grail." The small man sighed deeply and with passion, and a look of perfect ecstasy made his features shine.

"What?" Jack Lucas could not believe his ears.

"It's God's symbol of divine grace," the bearded man said very quietly and reverently.

This was too much, even for Jack. "The Holy Grail? Some billionaire has the Holy Grail sitting in his library on Fifth Avenue?" he demanded.

"I know! You can't imagine how surprised I was. Who would think you could find anything divine on the upper east side!"

That tore it. With his boots or without them, Jack was outta here. "Listen, I don't mean to enrage you or anything, but . . . I'm not the One. I'm not *any* One." He started to push past the small man, whose face paled in consternation.

"I think you're a very nice . . . very nice psychotic man," Jack continued, looking for the exit. "I really appreciate what you did for me. It was a very brave and noble thing—"

"Oh, please, you're embarrassing me—"

"I wish you all the luck in the world. When you get the Grail, I'm sure I'll be seeing lots of you on various talk shows."

Tears filled the bearded man's eyes. He became visibly agitated. "But I can't. . . . But I can't get it!" he cried, and ran over to the poster of the armed knight. Picking up the red marker, he began to add more crimson streaks to the man and the horse. His arm swept over the picture in frantic strokes. "He

. . . he's out there . . . I don't know if . . . He's always out there, see . . . and—'' He looked pleadingly at Jack. ''See, you don't know him, that's why you're the One . . . you can get it—''

''I'm not the One!'' Jack shouted. Then, in a more placating tone, he said, ''Listen, forget about the shoes. I'll just take a cab. Good-bye, uh—'' He suddenly realized he didn't know the fellow's name. No, wait a minute. What had that bum called him last night? ''Uh, Garry.''

''Parry,'' the small man corrected him quietly. He looked very disappointed, on the brink of tears.

''Parry. I'm Jack.''

''I know.'' It was obvious now that Jack was really going, so Parry ran to a little space behind the boiler and retrieved Jack's silver-capped boots. Picking up the Pinocchio doll, he handed doll and boots to Jack.

''Thanks,'' Jack said, taking the boots. ''You can keep the doll.''

''Thanks a million,'' Parry said gratefully, and his mood shifted. ''Now that you know where we are, don't be a stranger. And I'll give you a buzz and we'll get together and get this thing off the ground. Take care of yourself, Jack. Give my love to the wife.''

Halfway out the door, Jack turned. ''I'm not married,'' he said.

''Really? You look married.''

What kind of thing was that to say? It was an odd remark, even for Parry. In what way did he look married? Jack shook his head and, clutching his Tony Lamas tightly against his chest, made good his escape.

The door from the boiler room led out into the rest of the basement, which was lighted, clean, and well cared for. Jack had no idea where he was, but it had all the earmarks of a high-rent building. Which way out? Ahead of him, down a long hallway, he could see an exit door, which led, he presumed, to the stairs up to the lobby. His head still throbbing from the hangover, his burned hand starting to act up again, Jack pulled his boots on and headed for the exit.

"Hey, hey, where you comin' from?"

The sudden voice took him by surprise. Halfway up the stairs, Jack turned to see an irate black man heading toward him. The man wore coveralls with the name Frank stitched over the breast pocket. Obviously the superintendent, and he was steamed, mad as hell.

"Uh, basement, I think," answered Jack, acutely aware that he looked and smelled like any Bowery bum. He was unshaved, unwashed, uncombed, and filthy.

"I tell him *no visitors!*" yelled the super in the direction of the basement. "Who the hell are you and what are you doin' here?"

The loud voice cut right through Jack's aching head like a searing knife. He saw red spots dancing in front of his eyes and knew he had to get out of there before he was sick all over the stairs.

"Hey, hold it! Hold it!" Frank called after him. "You a friend of Parry's?"

Jack turned back. "No."

" 'Cause I don't allow no entertainin'. I let him stay here out of the goodness of my heart because of the tragedy, but this is no hotel and nobody's takin' advantage of me," Frank continued indignantly.

"Tragedy?" Jack asked.

Frank climbed the basement stairs until he was only one step away from Jack. He lowered his voice, more for dramatic effect than for confidentiality. "He an' his wife were in some bar . . . and some nut comes in with a shotgun and blew the place apart. Splattered her brains all over the walls. She never knew what hit her. You oughta heard about that. The nut who listened to the radio?''

Jack sank back against the wall of the staircase, his face a ghastly white. His heart was pumping so hard in his chest he could barely catch his breath. All he could think of was, Gotta get away from here. Gotta get home. I gotta get home.

Seven

Jack Lucas came out blinking into the street, his aching eyes blinded by the strong morning sunlight, and took a look around. He found himself standing under a canopy in front of a prewar rent-stabilized building on Central Park West in the mid-Eighties. By some miracle, there was still cab fare in the pocket of his jeans; after all his encounters of the previous evening, nobody had rolled him after all. It was tough getting a cab, though, because no sane driver would stop for a guy who looked like a Bowery bum. The way he succeeded at last was to jump into a taxi that had stopped for a red light. Before the driver could lock his doors or throw him out, Jack had waved a few greenbacks in his face and given the address of the Video Spot.

It was an agonizing drive back. Frank the superintendent's words kept resounding in Jack's ears like the dirgeful tolling of a bronze bell. *Never knew what hit her. That nut who listened to the radio.* And the sweet, insane face of a small man called Parry floated into Jack's brain like one of Parry's fat fairies, the Little People, a vision within sight but out of reach.

Parry. I did this to him, Jack thought in anguish. I killed the only person he loved. I made him crazy. It's my fault. This was a new aspect of his guilt, one he hadn't encountered before.

Apart from the gruesome sight on his television

screen that awful evening, Jack Lucas had never faced the actual physical presence of his and Edwin Malnick's victims. Their blood might have been on his hands, but not up in his face. Now this Parry was up in Jack's face—living, breathing, walking, talking, shooting rubber arrows, hallucinating. Living in a basement boiler room was the once sane palpable proof of Jack Lucas's terrible guilt.

For six months, ever since the senseless shootings, Jack Lucas had tallied the body count over and over in his head. Eight dead. Seven strangers and a pathetic psycho named Edwin Malnick. Eight. His sense of guilt could barely handle eight. But it hadn't occurred to him that there might be even more than eight. That there might be an entire regiment of the living dead, the people left behind to mourn. Like Parry. Like crazy Parry. Parry made nine. *Splattered her brains all over the wall. She was a beautiful girl. . . .*

And how many more than nine? Jack might never know, but he was surely as guilty of their misery as he was of Parry's madness. Unconsciously, Jack shrank back against the torn imitation leather of the taxi seat, wrapped his arms around his body, and whimpered. Salty tears squeezed out of his eyes. He wasn't even aware of doing it, but the taxi driver, taking a good look at his passenger in the rearview mirror, put his foot down hard on the gas pedal. The sooner this weeping wino was out of his cab, the better off he'd be. New York! Everybody was a mental case!

When Anne Napolitano first met Jack Lucas, she could see the black cloud hanging over his head. She knew he'd be trouble. He was a man haunted by a terrible misfortune, a man who'd lost every vestige of the good life and was trying to hide from his miseries in the bottom of a bottle. In short, the kind of man who needed the love of a strong and maternal woman. Anne the earth mother. Her favorite role. Without thinking twice, she jumped right into the relationship.

And he was trouble, lots of trouble, but up to recently he'd been worth it. He needed her, and he let her know it. Jack was a passionate, skillful, and enthusiastic lover, and Anne was hung up on his big, strong body. She loved the long dimples on both sides of his mouth, his deep-set, blue, brooding eyes, his intelligence and quick sardonic wit. In short, Anne Napolitano loved Jack Lucas, period.

But lately, things between them had been starting to go sour. Anne was a practical woman who saw things with a realistic eye. Yes, Jack had been through hell. Yes, Jack felt guilty about that terrible night at Babbitt's bar. Yes, a lot of innocent people had died. But Jack himself hadn't pulled the trigger, and no amount of guilt he felt could bring any of those men and women back to life. Guilt didn't put any butter on the bread of life. So why carry it around with you night and day? It was time already to stop brooding, time to start living. You can't go around forever with your chin hanging lower than your ass. It was way past time for Jack to snap out of it and get his shit together.

But Jack Lucas had shown no signs of snapping out of it. On the contrary, his consumption of alcohol had, if anything, increased lately. He seemed content just to vegetate with his bourbon and his ciggies, to let Anne take care of business and take care of him, to relinquish into her care all responsibility for his life. He'd become uncommunicative and unresponsive. Worse than that, as his bourbon consumption rose, hardly anything else did. Like many an alcoholic's, Jack's libido was decreasing at warp speed. No more enthusiasm. No more nibbles and secret kisses in hidden places. Lately he had to be coaxed to make love, sometimes even bribed. This hurt Anne terribly, making her feel unwanted and unattractive. The sex had been wonderful, a ten; now it was close to a zero.

Anne Napolitano was an outspoken woman whose language was the language of the streets of Brooklyn's Little Italy, a good but tough place to grow up. But underneath the surface of her frequently crude words flowed a deep well of wisdom and understanding. What she said was: "Jack, you're flying in smaller and smaller circles. Someday you'll fly up your own asshole and disappear." What she meant was: "Jack, you've got to let go of this obsessive self-absorption or someday you'll self-destruct." And what she meant was: "I care very deeply about what happens to you."

But caring didn't mean that Anne was going to let Jack use her as a doormat to wipe the mud off his fancy boots. Last night he hadn't come home; that had made her crazy, torn between fear for his safety and the near certainty that he was giving to another woman everything he was withholding from her. So when he turned up at last this morning, filthy, bleary-eyed, and stinking like a cross between a brewery, a filling station, and a sewer, Anne turned her face away from him and refused to talk to him. At first.

But Jack looked so miserable, sitting across from her in her crowded office at the back of the store, that Anne relented a little. Besides, one thing she couldn't do was stay silent for very long in any circumstances. Talk was her natural element; it was the air she breathed, the bread she ate, the wine she drank.

"Ya need to pick up a phone and let me know you're not dead," she reproached him. "Why couldn't ya do that?"

Before Jack could stammer out an answer, there

was a tap on the door, and Donna, a clerk at the Video Spot, put her head around it.

"What!" roared Anne, annoyed.

"A guy wants to check out the pornos," said Donna, waving at the wall of pornographic video-tapes behind Anne's desk.

"So send him back!" Then, turning to Jack, Anne's voice softened a little. "I need to know that you haven't been attacked, or raped, or God knows what! You disappear last night, I don't know what to think. I was up all night long! Look at you!"

The door opened, and a middle-aged man, neatly dressed in suit and tie, came into the office, and slightly embarrassed, began to peruse the titles on the wall.

"I can't tell you how distraught I was," Anne continued as though there were nobody else in the room with them. "All night long. What the hell happened?"

"I was attacked," Jack mumbled.

"What? Oh, baby," cried Anne. That was all she had to hear. Now she was all sympathy.

"Two kids tried to set me on fire." Jack held up his burned hand for her to see.

"*Oh, my God! What did they do? My God!*" Anne yelled, and got up hastily. She rushed around the desk and grabbed Jack, hugging him hard, making him wince in pain. The businessman stopped reading the porno titles; this little live drama was far more interesting than a videotape.

Pulling away from Anne, Jack jerked his head in the direction of the man and gave her a look that said plainly, Get this guy the hell out of here.

"Are you almost done?" she demanded brusquely, and the man jumped a little.

"I've seen most of these," he muttered defensively.

"Whaddya lookin' for, a story?" Reaching up,

Anne grabbed a tape off the shelf and thrust it at the man. "Here . . . *Creamer Versus Creamer* . . . it won an award. Go."

The guy grabbed the videotape and went. As soon as the door closed behind him Anne turned all her attention to Jack.

"You were attacked! My God, you want me to call the police? Should I call a doctor?"

"No . . . no, I'm fine, really." Jack shook his head, half-touched, half-amused by her concern.

She looked at him sharply, her eyes assessing him for damage. "You all right? You're sure?"

He nodded, and Anne moved along to what was really on her mind. She tried to keep her voice casual, but failed dismally.

"So . . . where did you sleep last night?"

Jack shifted uneasily in his chair. How could he possibly explain to her about Parry? "I . . . I stayed at a friend's. Anne, listen, I—"

But Anne put her hand up to cut him off. "Jack, Jack, I want you to be up-front with me now. If you're seein' somebody else, let me know. You don't have to pour gasoline on yourself and light a match just to break up with me. Just tell me the truth."

It was apparent to Jack that underneath the bravado of her words, Anne Napolitano was hurting. He owed her something. "Anne, I was not seeing anybody else. I really was attacked," he told her sincerely.

She threw him a look out of the corner of her eye and saw that he meant what he said. This brought on another spate of demonstrative sympathy, and she threw her arms around Jack and hugged him hard. Wincing, he pushed her away.

"I got a cut."

"Okay, I see it now. I'm sorry." But it was hard for her to let him go. She wanted to rock him in her arms until he felt better about life and about himself. Impossible wish; it would never happen.

"Okay," Anne said at last, moving away from Jack with a small shrug. "Whaddya gonna do? I love you."

She waited for his reply, but none came. "You don't have to say it back." She sighed. "Although it wouldn't break your jaw. Go, go upstairs and take your bath. I'll cook tonight."

He couldn't shake the thought of Parry, or his desperate feelings of owing him something that he could never repay. All day long, while Anne worked downstairs in her video store, Jack Lucas thought about Parry. He thought about Parry while he bathed and dressed and brushed his teeth and napped and drank some bourbon and smoked some cigarettes and brooded over the events of the night before.

Jack could visualize Parry quite clearly in his memory—small, brave, even gallant, cheerful, insane. Again and again Jack remembered how Parry had saved his life, how he'd nurtured him, and why. To explain to Jack his mission for God. The "Janitor of God" he'd called himself, this lunatic visionary on a chivalric quest to find the Holy Grail. How crazy can you get? In the 1990s, in New York City, somewhere in the mansion of a billionaire, locked away behind burglar-proof glass, was kept the very same cup that Jesus Christ had drunk from at the Last Supper.

Yeah, right. And yet Parry believed it with his entire childlike soul.

Anne's lasagna was delicious, but Jack ate it without tasting it. He might as well have been eating cardboard. He was unaware, too, that Anne was keeping an eye on him, disturbed by his brooding silence and his preoccupation.

As she stood up to clear away the dinner dishes, Jack asked suddenly, "You know what the Holy Grail is?"

"The Holy Grail? Yeah, I know that one. It was like . . . Jesus' juice glass." When Jack stared at her, surprised, Anne added with a crooked smile, "Oh, yeah, I used to be such a Catholic." There was the merest tinge of regret in her words, as though she felt a stirring of longing for those simpler, purer times.

"You still believe in God?" Jack asked.

"Oh, sure, gotta believe in God." Anne set the dishes on the table and sat back down. Her forehead wrinkled with effort as she struggled to put her beliefs into words. Anne Napolitano wasn't used to wrestling with philosophical issues.

"But I don't think God made man in his own image. No. 'Cause most of the shit that happens is because of men. No, I think man was made in the devil's image and women were created out of God. Because women can have babies, which is sorta like creating, and which also accounts for the fact that women are so attracted to men. Because—let's face it—the devil is a helluva lot more interesting."

She lit a cigarette and puffed deeply on it, then let it dangle from the corner of her lips as she continued. "I slept with a few saints, and believe me, I know what I'm talking about. Boooooring! And so the whole point of life, I think, is for men and women to get married so that the devil and God can get together and work it out." Standing up, Anne shifted the cigarette and moved over to Jack for a kiss. "Not that we have to get married or anything. God f-bid!" She uttered a short, unconvincing laugh.

Jack couldn't help himself; he shrank away from her ever so slightly, yet enough for Anne to notice. In the last month or so, if she'd mentioned marriage once, she must have mentioned it a hundred times.

She was beginning to harp on it, and it really turned him off. Besides, as she loomed over him now, he noticed something unappetizing on her face, a blemish on her chin. That turned him off, too.

"You . . . have a little . . . uh . . . something on your face."

Anne pulled away, embarrassed. Instinctively, her hand went up to hide the eyesore from his view. "Oh, I got a pimple. This stuff is supposed to blend with my skin color. Like it really works, y'know."

Standing up from his chair, Jack dodged around Anne and went over to the little makeshift bar to pour himself another drink. Anne came up behind him and coyly removed the glass from his hand and set it down. Jack groaned inwardly; he knew what this meant. It was her signal. She wanted to play.

"I . . . don't think I'm up to it tonight, honey," he began, but Anne was busy massaging his shoulders. "I just had a very traumatic experience."

She nodded to show she heard him, but her hands were making larger circles on his shoulders, then down along his spine to his hips.

"Ow, ow, ow . . ." Jack pleaded, trying and failing to free himself from her forceful fingers. "I think I'm getting sick. . . . Anne, I spent the night in a boiler room. . . . Anne, I'm tired. . . . I'm upset. . . . I'm just not in the mood . . . okay?"

"Okay," she agreed, leaning her weight against him and pushing him down on the sofa. Then she climbed over him, mounting him and pushing her tongue deeply into his mouth, still caressing him with circular movements of her strong hands. Pressing herself against him, Anne began to undo the buttons of his shirt.

It was too much for Jack. It would be easier simply to give in than to fight her. Besides, he was starting to enjoy it. He could feel the warmth of her opulent body under her tight blouse and skirt, and it was getting to him. He felt himself responding. With a little moan, half of passion, half of resignation, Jack pushed Anne to the floor, and they began to make love.

Afterward, released, his energy spent along with his passion, Jack was able to explain to Anne about Parry, about the mad young man whose wife was blown away in front of his eyes and whose reaction was to leave reality behind. While she held him, saying nothing, silent tears streaming down her cheeks, Jack told her in a low voice of the sorry knight and the insanity of his impossible quest.

It was when he got to the part about his refusal of a role in the quest, and his running out on Parry, that Jack Lucas broke down and cried.

Eight

When he woke up the following morning, Jack Lucas found himself still haunted. He was as haunted by this man Parry as Parry himself was by his hallucinatory vision of the Holy Grail. He couldn't get Parry out of his mind. Like the Ancient Mariner in the poem. He shot a seabird whom the sailors considered lucky and was forced to go around forever with the albatross tied around his neck. Having destroyed Henry Sagan's mind, Jack was now forced to carry the burden of Parry's insanity.

All he knew was that he had to learn more about his personal albatross, the man whose wife had been blown away in front of his eyes. Reluctantly, fearing another encounter with the divine madness that infused Parry's brain, Jack took himself over to the apartment building on Central Park West.

He made his way cautiously down the steps from the lobby to the basement and knocked on the boiler-room door. No answer. Jack pushed the door open. Empty. No Parry. Oddly, Jack felt a twinge of disappointment mingling with his relief. He didn't want to meet him, yet strangely, some part of him wanted to see Parry again.

Jack stepped inside and looked around curiously at Parry's ''neck of the woods,'' searching for clues to the mystery of the bearded man. The first thing he noticed was that Parry had taken the little Pinocchio doll and set it up against the back wall as a kind of never-sleeping guardian of his sanctuary. Funny, it looked right at home there, its painted eyes wide open as though he were guarding the portals of the underworld, that happy smile permanently on its little face.

There were the books, of course; Jack went to these first. He himself was college-educated and he considered himself well read, but almost all of the titles here were unfamiliar to him. They all dealt with the Middle Ages—history, literature, weaponry, religion, daily life, chivalry, the Crusades, Arthurian legend, the Holy Grail. Pulling the Grail book off the makeshift shelf, Jack quickly skimmed over the pages dealing with the Christian legend of the quest by the knights of the Round Table.

It all came back to him now. The Grail was believed to provide an unending source of nourishment and healing; it cured all wounds, no matter how grave, because it embodied God's boundless grace. The legend goes that during the Crucifixion of Jesus, Joseph of Arimathea caught some of the Lord's blood in the sacred vessel and escaped with the Grail to England. It provided him with sustenance all his life and was handed down to his descendants for many generations. At last it disappeared, and thus became the object of a quest by King Arthur's best knights. The holy vessel could be found only by one who was totally pure in heart and mind. Only Sir Galahad, Joseph of Arimathea's last descendant, ever achieved the Grail. His strength was as the strength of ten, because his heart was pure. Sir Percival also completed the quest and was rewarded by the sight of the Holy Grail.

And this symbol of purity and divinity, this stuff of legends, this unattainable and mystical ideal was the very cup that Parry believed he saw in a glossy eight-dollar architectural magazine. Jack shook his head at the many and varied forms dementia takes.

He left the books and walked around Parry's tiny quarters. The small table held a large piece of paper, rolled up. Jack unrolled it and saw with surprise that it was a hand-drawn map, evidently of Langdon Carmichael's armory and the city blocks surrounding it. Nervously, Jack rolled it back up and turned his attention to the walls.

Most of the pictures had been ripped out of Parry's books and taped to the wall. As Jack studied the pictures carefully he could perceive a kind of pattern emerging, a delineation of the medieval parameters of Parry's delusion. There was an iconlike quality to the pictures, a worshipful celebration of chivalry and beauty. But on the opposing wall, the red-marked picture of the monstrous Red Knight, his wickedly sharp lance exploding in flame, the hooves of his war-horse pounding directly at the viewer, seemed to personify the inescapable evil of the world.

There was something chilling about the Red Knight. Jack shivered a little and moved into the alcove, where Parry kept his mysterious shrine. This time, without Parry here to stop him, he was able to look more closely at the strange objects on the altar.

In addition to the Chinese-food container and the romance novel, he saw a package of jawbreakers, a plastic flower, some cheap but glittery earrings—everything arranged carefully as an offering. In the center, with votive candles in front of it, was the picture of the beautiful maiden. She had long, flowing golden hair and a soft, sweet, virginal other-worldly smile. Whoever she was supposed to represent, Jack could tell she was the object of Parry's veneration. His dead wife? The Virgin Mary? The lady fair in peril of the dragon? But this other stuff on the altar, what did it mean? He didn't get it. He didn't get any of it.

''Can I help you?'' The voice was sharp and sud-

den, making Jack jump. He turned to see Frank, the
building superintendent, glaring at him.

"I . . . I'm just looking for Parry."

"He's not here." The man stood waiting for Jack
to leave, but Jack wasn't ready to leave. He needed
to know more, to find some key to the puzzle of this
room and its enigmatic contents, and especially to
the man who made his home here.

"What did you say his name used to be?" Jack
asked. There was supplication in his eyes.

Frank hesitated, looking Jack up and down. Then
he nodded, deciding to trust him, and left the boiler
room, gesturing for Jack to follow. His superintendent's apartment was down the basement hall, and
he unlocked the door and beckoned Jack inside.
From a closet he took down a large duffel bag and
began to take Parry's things out of it for Jack to look
at.

Here, tumbling out of a canvas bag, was the sum
and substance of a sane man's life. It was a small
collection of objects, but significant. There were two
framed certificates of master's degrees in medieval
literature and medieval history.

"That's his real name, Henry Sagan," said Frank,
pointing to the degrees. "He was a teacher over at
Hunter College. They kept him in some mental place
over on Staten Island. He didn't say a word for over
a year . . . then, all of a sudden, he starts talkin',
only now he's this Parry guy."

Fascinated, Jack pawed through Parry's things.
Here was a snapshot taken of him in Central Park.
Here was the sane Parry, whose name was not Parry
but Henry Sagan. He stood smiling into the camera,
his short hair ruffled a little in the breeze, his beard
neatly trimmed, his clothing exactly what you'd expect from an academic, a teacher of medieval history—button-down shirt with a Shetland sweater
pulled over it under a favorite old tweed jacket. The

eyes glowed with humor and intelligence . . . and sanity. It was painful for Jack to see it, and he put the picture down and picked up a thick sheaf of paper bound neatly into a folder. He opened it to the title page.

The Fisher King: A Mythic Journey for Modern Man
Doctoral Thesis by Henry Sagan.

"He and his wife used to live upstairs," Frank continued. "So when he got released, they sent him here. I felt bad. He couldn't work. Nobody wanted him. So I let him stay in the basement. He helps out, I give him a couple of dollars. People throw things away, he gets them."

Jack picked up a wedding ring and turned it in his hands, putting it back hurriedly as though it had burned his fingers. Then he lifted a photograph of a woman and studied it. The young woman in the picture was radiant. Although her features were close to perfect and she was very pretty by any standards, there was something more than prettiness in her laughing face. There was tenderness and sweetness and warmth, and a brilliance that came up from within. Jack could understand easily how Henry Sagan must have loved her. He shuddered at the thought of Edwin Malnick's bullets tearing through that head, of the blood and brains that must have welled up over that tumbled light brown hair.

"She was a beautiful girl," said Frank sadly. "He was crazy about her."

It was finally too much. Jack couldn't take another minute of this. He'd learned all he wanted, and more besides. He was choking on his new knowledge; it was a fire in his chest that threatened to engulf him.

Jack tossed in bed for hours, but sleep eluded him, mocking him for even trying. Beside him in the large bed, Anne slept soundly, the sweet, untroubled rest of one whose conscience is clear. At last Jack gave up the struggle. He slipped out of bed and left the bedroom in his underwear. Padding barefoot across the living room, he snapped on only one light, a table lamp. Semidarkness ought to be enough for a haunted man.

Moving slowly, as though he were very old, he pulled his scrapbooks and his tapes off the shelf in the living room and piled them up on the floor. He turned on Anne's portable cassette player and put in a tape of one of his radio shows, selected at random.

Any old tape; what was the difference? They were all pretty much alike. Jack Lucas on top, the callers on the bottom. The Superstar meets the Bungled and the Botched. As the tape played he heard the eager voices of his fans and his own bored and confident voice answering them in that superior tone he always affected to impress them. Oh, he'd given them attitude, all right! Fuck 'em all, save six for pallbearers. Jack Lucas's personal philosophy of life.

But Jack soon lost interest; he wasn't really listening, anyway. He just needed to hear a tape of his show as background noise, as an audible reminder of what used to be. He sat down on the floor, turning the pages of the scrapbooks, rereading the clippings that marked the progress of his successes—the stories in *Billboard* and *Radio & Records* and *Variety,* the reviews of his program in the New York papers, the press releases and glossy photos sent out by the station to hype the *Jack Lucas Morning Show.* A strong feeling of nostalgia tempered his melancholy. It really was as good as he remembered it. He'd led an enviable life. He missed it terribly.

But soon he came to the yellowing front pages that screamed in sensational headlines the shootings at Babbitt's. His own name in thick black letters six inches high, a better billing even than Edwin's. Jack's hand trembled, but he still kept turning pages. There was Edwin Malnick's face looking up at him, as much victim as killer. Edwin, who didn't have an original thought in his head until Jack Lucas had put one terrible one there. Jack shuddered, remembering, regretting, wishing only that he could turn back the hands of time, unsay the words he had said, make those people come back to life, go on living his old life. If only Edwin Malnick hadn't taken him literally! He closed the scrapbook and set it aside.

A sudden shaft of light came in from the bedroom and slanted across the floor, hitting Jack. Anne Napolitano, her bathrobe wrapped around her, walked into the living room with a cigarette in her hand.

"Whatsa matter, hon, can't sleep?" she asked sympathetically. Jack's tapes had wakened her; her voice was still thick with sleepiness.

Jack didn't look up. He was sitting as still as if he were carved out of stone.

"I tell you something, Anne," he said at last in a shaky voice. "I really feel like I'm cursed. I get the feeling like I'm . . . a magnet, but I attract shit. Out of all the people in this city, why did I meet a man whose wife I killed?"

It was an unanswerable question. Anne's big heart went out to him. She knelt down close to Jack and touched his shoulder with a gentle hand. "You didn't kill anybody. Stop it."

Jack shook his head. "I wish there was some way I could . . . just . . . pay the fine and go home." His voice broke, and he could say no more.

This was the most honest thing he'd ever said to her. Anne slipped one arm around him, and he turned and buried his face in her breast, clutching her to him very tightly. Anne held him with both arms now, hugging him hard, while Jack wept against her body, his shoulders shaking with deep, convulsive sobs. She could feel his tears burning her breasts.

"I know, honey, I know . . . shhh . . . shhhh," she whispered, rocking him in her arms as though he were her own crying child. Anne had never loved Jack as much as she loved him this moment, when he allowed her to look into and pity the black depths of his pain and vulnerability. If only she could hold on tight and never let him go!

Jack left the house early the following day and took the subway and a crosstown bus down to the Manhattan Bridge, looking for Parry. He had something to give him, something to make Parry's life better and ease Jack's guilty conscience a little. If he succeeded, then maybe he'd never have to deal with Parry again.

There were fewer homeless people under the abutment during the day, but Jack soon found Parry's little band of brethren—the Irishman, the black man, and the hippie kid. Of Parry himself, there was no sign.

The guys didn't recognize him at first, because Jack looked so different from the other night. He was sober, for one thing. For another, Jack was clean, shaved, and dressed neatly in fresh clothes. They didn't want to talk to him, and they particularly didn't want to tell him where Parry could be found. But the burn bandage on Jack's hand convinced them of his identity and allowed them to be less paranoid.

"So where can I find Parry?"

"You know the Haagensen Building?" asked the black man.

"On Twenty-Fourth and Madison? That big office building?" Jack countered, surprised.

"That's the place. You can find Parry outside there every weekday. Not on Saturday or Sunday, though. Today a weekday?"

"Yes," said Jack, and it occurred to him that men like these didn't live by clocks or calendars. If anything, time was their enemy. Time had stolen away their years without giving anything back. Time mocked their days and evenings, dragging them out as they hunted like sewer rats for survival.

"Then for sure he's there. But you gotta get there before twelve, or you won't find him."

Jack looked at his watch: 11:35. He had to hustle if he was going to make it. "Thanks." Digging into his pocket for a few bills, he handed them around. Somewhere in his memory, he seemed to hear himself saying to somebody, "A couple of quarters isn't going to make any difference anyway." When had he thought that? Maybe a thousand years ago, give or take a century.

Jack set off uptown in search of Parry. The Haagensen Building, every weekday. What was he doing there?

Nine

Jack climbed out of the Lexington Avenue subway at the Twenty-third Street station with four minutes to spare. He was going to make this fast and get it over with once and for all; a simple cash transaction and then good-bye forever. Anne was right; he couldn't carry this shitload of guilt around with him all his days.

As he approached the Haagensen Building Jack could see Parry, sitting on the roof of a car across the avenue from the skyscraper, his eye fixed to the clock in the tower. He was mumbling under his breath as Jack approached him. Jack couldn't hear most of the words, but he did make out "sovereign princess," "faithful slave," and "who endures such misery for love of thee." The guy was rambling on again.

"Parry!" he called in greeting.

"Hi, Jack," Parry answered without taking his eyes off the clock. It was now less than a minute to noon.

Jack came to the point without preamble. "Hey, listen," he said, rummaging in his pockets. "I thought maybe you could use a couple of bucks."

At that very moment the hands of the clock came together, and a loud, sonorous tolling of the noon-hour bells split the air. Agile as lightning, Parry leaped off the car and grabbed hold of Jack.

"Come on!" he yelled urgently, and half dragged

Jack into traffic and across the avenue to the building. He stopped about six or seven yards away from the revolving doors, with a good view of them, and a breathless and puzzled Jack Lucas came to a halt beside him.

The Haagensen Building is one of New York's great art-deco structures, built in the booming market and optimistic prosperity of the 1920s. It boasts a marble lobby, carved stone, and beautiful deco ironwork inside and out, and its impressive lobby is reached by means of heavy bronze revolving doors. Parry's eyes were glued to the revolving doors. Above their heads, from the building's clock towers, the noon hour was still ringing.

Now that the workday lunch hour had officially arrived, the revolving doors were turning busily as the men and women who worked in the building came streaming out for a meal and a midday break.

"Look, look," Parry whispered urgently. And Jack looked. He saw a bunch of people coming through the doors into the street, and one skinny girl not quite making it. Too slightly built to deal with the weight of the doors and the eager impatience of the people behind and ahead of her, she got revolved right back into the lobby.

"She'll be back," said Parry with confidence.

And, a few seconds later, she was back, out on the street at last, straightening her woolen beret that had become dislodged in her struggle with the revolving door.

"Ahhhhh, there she is, see her?" Parry murmured with passion.

Jack Lucas looked in the direction of his ardent gaze, and his eyes widened in surprise. Nobody, nobody even not in his right mind could call this young woman a beauty. First of all, she was too thin. Jack's own personal taste ran in favor of thin women, but he liked tall, willowy women, with legs that went all the way up to their armpits. This girl was small and scrawny, like an underfed chicken.

She wore a man-tailored suit two sizes too large for her so that she virtually disappeared inside her clothing, as though her garments were her hiding place. The suit was drab and seemed to be made out of that dark-colored iron-hard fabric that you see on Soviet leaders. More than anything, she resembled a child dressed up in her grandmother's clothing.

The girl's face was plain, with a large nose and short hair of no particular color that she kept tucked up inside her woolen beret. The beret, which can make a rakish statement on a person of style, was pulled down formlessly over her head like a cooking pot. She had no makeup on, so her face was pale and her features without definition. The young woman wore thick-soled "sensible" shoes on her feet, but she didn't walk with ease or confidence. Instead, she sidled and stumbled along clumsily, occasionally bumping into someone and mouthing silent apologies. When she bumped into the lamppost on the corner, she apologized to that, too. A timid soul if ever Jack saw one.

"Isn't she a vision?" Parry breathed. There was no mistaking the dopey look on his face for anything but perfect love. Parry looked like a teenager with his first big crush. He obviously worshiped this awkward sparrow of a girl.

"Yeah, gorgeous. Look, I'm going. I just wanted to give you—" Jack began digging in his pocket again, but Parry was off and running, dodging behind the lunchtime crowd to stay out of the girl's sight, yet never taking his eyes off her. Impatient and annoyed, Jack followed.

The two of them stopped at the next corner, to watch the young woman select a book from the paperback rack attached to the newspaper stand. Selecting one book, she knocked down three. When she picked those three up from the sidewalk, she knocked down two more. At last she did manage to pull it all together and get her wallet out and pay for the book without further damage. As she tucked the book away into her old lady's black leather handbag Jack and Parry could read the title. It was the same kind of florid romantic junk that Anne loved so much, all cleavage and heavy breathing.

"She buys a new book every two days," Parry informed Jack. *"Love's Lost Found.* She's into trash. Whaddya gonna do?" He grinned fondly.

The girl, yawing off balance like a small ship in a large gale, went listing down the avenue and finally made port in a nearby Chinese restaurant, where she took a table. Immediately, Parry pressed his nose against the restaurant window so that he could see her every move. Both men watched as she ordered nervously. In less than two minutes her order was plunked down in front of her in a domed metal dish with a knob on the cover. Taking the cover off, Parry's lady fair managed to burn her fingers and drop the lid into the dish. There was a big splash and dumpling juice mixed with soy sauce splattered all over the tablecloth.

"Awww, she loves dumplings," Parry purred. "It's her Wednesday ritual."

Jack shifted impatiently from foot to foot. He was determined to get this over with, give Parry a little money, and get the hell out of his life. He had enough albatrosses hanging around his neck as it was, without adding a mental case. In New York, money solves almost anything. It was never Jack's intention to go trotting down Fourth Avenue in Parry's tow, dogging the footsteps of some homely waif who didn't even seem to know that she was the focus of a crazy man's fantasies. The sooner he was out of here, the better.

But Parry's attention was not to be diverted. This

was the high point of his day, the hour he lived for, when he could actually see his lady love dropping a slippery Chinese dumpling off her chopsticks and into her lap. His eyes squeezed shut in rapture.

"That's so sweet," he murmured to Jack. "She does that every time." He appeared to find every gaffe this graceless young person committed irresistibly adorable.

The couple sitting at the window table had been growing more and more uncomfortable at having to confront the faces of two men staring in at them, particularly when one of them had his nose pressed so tightly against the glass that his features were grotesquely distorted. Angrily, they rapped on the window and made superior little waving-away gestures with their hands.

"We're looking through the window!" Jack roared. "You got some problem with that, buddy? We're looking through the fuckin' window!"

Why was he overreacting so angrily? Partly because he was embarrassed to be caught in this Peeping Tom situation, partly because it was humiliating to be identified, even by strangers, as a bum and a companion of bums. But also, buried somewhere deep, there was perhaps a small core of protectiveness toward Parry that Jack himself didn't recognize. Who were these people to act so goddamn superior, to decree that Parry couldn't look into a restaurant window? Even the craziest bum should have rights.

While his young lady was paying her bill, Parry grabbed Jack again and rushed him away from the restaurant, to a vantage point nearby where they could watch her leaving and follow her back to her office. Any other young woman might have noticed that she was being followed, because it really was something of a circus parade with Parry only yards behind her and Jack trotting angrily after Parry, but this girl didn't seem to be able to tell night from day, or rain from sunshine.

She didn't go directly back to work, but stopped at the newsstand again, this time to drop her purse and buy a package of brightly colored jawbreakers.

"If anybody ever told me I'd be in love with a woman who eats jawbreakers," Parry confided to Jack as they witnessed the purchase from five feet away, "I'd say they were nuts. But look at that jaw!"

It all fell into place now. The jawbreakers, the Chinese-food containers, the love novel—all votive objects placed lovingly on the altar in a shrine in Parry's little boiler room. A shrine dedicated to a pale, unpretty, awkward young woman who didn't even know he existed.

In his mind's eye Jack could see the beautiful portrait of the Botticelli flower maiden with her flowing golden locks. This was how Parry idealized his love, this must be how he perceived this graceless girl he was following like a dog. Jack didn't know whether to laugh or to cry, but if he needed any more proof of Parry's total insanity, he had it right here in Parry's romantic obsession.

Now the girl was trying to get back to work, past the dragons that guarded the revolving doors. It wasn't easy; she kept being brushed aside by other workers moving in and out, but finally she positioned herself so that she was caught up in the moving stream and pulled into the building. She disappeared from sight.

"There she goes," said Parry wistfully, his heart in his eyes.

"Do you follow her every day?" Jack asked curiously.

Parry blushed, and his blue eyes looked sheepish. "It's not like that. I'm deeply smitten."

"Who is she? What's her name?"

Parry looked a little startled, as though he'd never

considered the question. "I don't know," he confessed. "Oh, look! A cooler! Wow!"

He broke away from Jack and ran to a mound of rubbish piled up against the curb. On top of the heap was a discarded Styrofoam cooler that Parry eagerly examined. It had a big hole in the bottom. "Needs a little work," he admitted out loud, but he was still delighted with his new possession. A cooler! His lucky day.

This was the moment Jack had been angling for; maybe now he could get Parry's undivided attention, if such a thing existed. He pulled some money from his pocket, selected a fifty-dollar bill, and held it out to Parry.

"Here. I . . . just . . . would like to help you. I thought maybe you could use some money."

Parry just stared at the bill, making no move to take it. "Fifty dollars?"

Jack misunderstood; he thought that it wasn't enough; Parry wanted more. Digging into his pocket again, he pulled out another bill, his last folding money. "Here's another twenty. Will that do?"

"Seventy dollars?" Totally dumbfounded, Parry looked at the money in Jack's outstretched hand.

Once again, Jack misread the situation. Not enough. Scowling, he sorted through the change from his pockets. "I mean, what's it going to take?"

At last Parry comprehended that the money was for him, a gift from Jack, and he was overcome by Jack's generosity. He lifted the fifty delicately from Jack's hand, leaving the twenty behind.

"No . . . no . . . it's . . . I don't know what to say! This is so nice of you, Jack."

Throwing his arms around Jack, Parry gave him a big hug, filled with gratitude and affection. Embarrassed half to death to be seen hugging a derelict on a New York City street, Jack pulled himself away from the embrace.

"That's okay," he mumbled. He was endlessly relieved that the moment had come and gone. He'd given Parry a little something; he was off the hook now. He wouldn't be haunted any more.

"You're a mensch, Jack. Can I take you to lunch?"

"No, I've got to get back to work. Take care of yourself." He turned away, a free man. No more Ancient Mariner.

At the corner, the light was red. Waiting for it to change, Jack glanced back over his shoulder at Parry. What he saw made him turn pale.

Another homeless man had set up a kind of shelter in the lee of the Haagensen building. He had a shopping cart piled high with a useless clutter of possessions, chief of which was a broken, disconnected telephone. In an earlier life, he'd been a stockbroker, a man who'd taken one high-wire walk too many without a net. When the market plunged, he'd plunged with it, down into madness. Now he spent his days on a telephone call to nowhere, reaching out to touch no one, issuing his orders to "Sell, sell, sell!"

What Jack saw, disbelieving, was Parry walking up to this cemento and handing over the fifty-dollar bill.

A new world of business opened up magically. "Buy! Buy! Buy!" yelled the bum.

"Hey! Hey!" yelled Jack, hotfooting it back.

"Well," Parry was advising the other man, "I think you should be realistic. You can't start an ad agency on fifty dollars." Three totally different people living in three totally different worlds.

"What are you doing?" Jack hollered at Parry, grabbing at the fifty in the other bum's hand. "Give that back!"

A small scuffle took place in which the desperate bum managed to hold on to the money, while Parry tugged at Jack until he got him away. The two men began to move up the street, Jack Lucas still not resigned to the loss of his money and the futility of his gesture. Now he was back on square one with his albatross, and out fifty bucks in the bargain.

"Why did you do that?" cried Jack, utterly frustrated. "I gave that money to you!"

"Well, what am *I* gonna do with it?" Parry asked, puzzled, as though it were the most rational question in the world.

Defeated, Jack shrugged. "I don't know. But I gave it to you, to help *you,* not him!"

Parry stopped and turned to look up at Jack. A mischievous little smile tugged at the corners of his mouth, spread across his face as a grin and wound up shining out of his bright blue eyes. There was a look of cunning on his face.

"You really want to help me?" he asked softly.

No. No, no, nonononono. He wasn't going to get suckered into this, vowed Jack. Nothing would make him get involved in this nutty Grail quest hallucination of Parry's. Nothing. No amount of guilt was going to make Jack Lucas even venture into the neighborhood of Langdon Carmichael's Fifth Avenue mansion. Nothing.

Ten

So, naturally, that's exactly where the two of them ended up, on Seventy-fourth Street and Fifth Avenue, right across the street from Langdon Carmichael's wonderful ten-million-big-ones armory. Jack Lucas had been dragged there kicking and screaming. Not literally, of course, because he was more than a head taller than Parry and must have outweighed him by a good forty pounds. But figuratively, he'd been blackmailed into it, because he knew he owed this crazy little man. Although not this much. Nobody owed anybody this much.

Still, Jack had gone along with the gag long enough to come and look. That was all Parry asked of him, to take a look-see. At least, that's all Parry was asking *now*. But he kept upping the ante. Inside that demented little head there seemed to be a peach pit of sane calculation that recognized that he had a hold of some kind over Jack and wouldn't hesitate to use it. A knight on a quest is wise to employ every weapon put at his disposal.

As they were turning the corner onto Fifth Avenue Parry made Jack shut his eyes, no peeking. He wanted the twentieth-century abode of the Holy Grail to come as a surprise to Jack.

And a surprise it was, no shit.

"Okay, you can open your eyes now," said Parry.

Jack Lucas opened his eyes. And blinked in amazement. The layout in the architectural magazine could not begin to suggest just how impressive the red-stone building really was. For one thing, it was a city block long and four stories high, with watchtowers at the corners of the roof. Built in the 1880s, during the art-nouveau period's reflowering of the Arthurian legend, the armory was erected like a medieval battlement to withstand an assault by the centuries. In style, it resembled closely a color print of a twelfth-century Norman castle out of a boy's book by Howard Pyle.

Instead of windows, there were narrow arrow slits, through which archers could shoot. The roof was topped by crenellations, little parapets of stone that would shield the defenders of the castle as they poured boiling oil down on the besiegers. There was a drawbridge with downward-pointing spikes, although its location on upper Fifth Avenue precluded a moat, which must have disappointed the architects no end. It had been designed as a fortress, it endured more than a hundred years as a fortress, and today it was even more of a fortress.

Impregnable as the structure was by nature, modern technology had made it more so. The arrow-slit windows, so thin that a plump cat couldn't squeeze through them, had been covered with protective bars. Sophisticated laser security systems in every room of the house connected directly to the local police station. It was termed, accurately, "immediate response." Wherever you went inside the house, even in the six luxurious bathrooms, a little red electronic eye followed you, and highly developed miniaturized video cameras surveilled you for posterity.

The Holy Grail might not be in Langdon Carmichael's library, but damn near everything else of value was, including priceless Renaissance objects by Benvenuto Cellini, a Rembrandt drawing, several Picassos, and a magnificent Monet flower painting, which cost as much as a small country, and which

Carmichael had acquired recently in a hailstorm of publicity. So there was plenty there to protect, and no expense had been spared in the protecting. A cockroach wouldn't have a Chinaman's chance of getting in there without setting off the alarms.

"Pretty impressive, huh?" Parry said proudly after Jack had stood there for two minutes saying nothing. "Don't let it scare you. Formidable as it seems, everything has its weakness."

"You can't just break into Langdon Carmichael's house," Jack protested. "This man has done nothing."

"Hey, I'll *deal* with it!" Parry retorted angrily. Evidently, he'd given some thought to the innocent-bystander aspect of his quest, and it still affected him like an exposed nerve. "Jack, just let me go through this one more time. The Holy Grail is in—"

"Listen to me!" Jack yelled, out of patience. This gag had gone as far as it was going to. "Don't start drooling, or rolling your eyes when I tell you this, but you shouldn't be doing this. There *is* no Holy Grail."

Parry chuckled, a rich baritone sound. "Oh, Jack, ye of little faith," he chided with affection. "There *has* to be a Grail. What do you think the Crusaders were, the pope's publicity stunt? Oh, you heathen! There's a Grail, come on!"

But Jack interrupted him. "Wait! Wait! Wait! Look, you're only partly insane. People like you can lead seminormal lives. You could get a job—"

"I have a job, Jack," said Parry earnestly. "I have a quest."

Jack ground his teeth in frustration. There was no reasoning with this maniac. It was like discussing philosophy with a gerbil, or trying to get a good fistfight going with a Mallomar. All one-sided. It made him crazy.

"I take it back!" he shouted, balling his hands

into fists. "You're fucking deranged! And you're going to get yourself killed trying to get in there!"

Parry took a step backward and looked up at Jack, and a sudden gasp of realization issued from his lips. His face suddenly radiated joy.

"Now I know what you're trying to do," he breathed happily. "You're trying to protect me, aren't you? You think there's danger—"

"No," snapped Jack. "I think you're a moron and I don't want to get into trouble."

But there was no convincing Parry. "You care!" he cried ecstatically, and he ran forward to throw his arms around Jack. For a small man he had surprising strength, and he hugged like a bear. "First the money, and now this! You care! Oh, you fabulous guy!"

Jack struggled furiously, but he couldn't break Parry's hold without hurting him, and he didn't want to hurt him. He just wanted him to see reason.

"Oh, you jaded and apathetic city!" Parry crowed, raising his voice for all of New York to hear. "I love this guy, do you hear me? I love this guy! He cares!"

This was too much for Jack, and he pushed Parry away vigorously. "Will you shut up!" he hissed in a choked, angry voice, looking around anxiously to make sure that nobody was watching.

But Parry was completely carried away by his emotion, and now his crow became a shout. "I love this man! You hear me, jaded city? I'm loopy about this guy! You're a real human being, Jack," he yelled loud enough to be heard six city blocks away.

Passersby were beginning to look now, and some of them laughed while others crossed the street so they wouldn't have to walk by the pair. Jack Lucas felt the hairs on his neck prickling. "Will you shut up!!" he growled.

Parry smiled. "You're a true friend."

That stung. "Believe me, I'm not," Jack said in a low voice. "I'm scum."

"I'm not going to listen to this. You're a real honest-to-goodness good guy."

"I'm self-centered, I'm weak," Jack went on, meaning it. "I don't have the willpower of a fly on shit."

"That's why the Little People sent you," Parry said happily. "They knew that. Magic is like that."

The irrationality of it all was beginning to get to Jack, to burn his circuits out. Here he was trying to have a normal conversation with Woody Woodpecker. "I don't believe in little floating people," he growled. "Okay? *There is no magic!*"

Jack's lack of faith rolled right off Parry's back. He'd come around. "You're going to help me. That's what matters," he answered with sunny confidence.

That blew it. Jack reached out and grabbed Parry by the shoulders. Here was a guy whose reality check had bounced twice and was no longer negotiable. Jack Lucas was determined to get reality across to him if he had to force-feed it down Parry's throat. It was for his own good, he told himself, so that the little guy wouldn't get hurt trying to make his delusions into realities. Actually, he was doing it so that his own guilt might be eased somewhat.

"Listen to me, Parry, or whatever your name is. You know none of this is true—not the Grail . . . not the voices. There's a part of you that knows it's not true!"

"I think we have to start planning now," said Parry, refusing to listen.

"I know who you are—" Jack insisted.

A look of panic entered Parry's eyes, his hands trembled, and he began to pull away. "Jack, come on . . . what are you saying? I know who you are? You're acting . . . really weird—"

'Or who you were. You don't belong on the streets. You're an intelligent man. You're a teacher—''

''No! No! No! . . . Jack! No!'' Parry was struggling now like a little wild animal trying to get out of a trap. Every word of Jack's was a spike being driven into his head. The pain, the pain was . . . agonizing . . . he couldn't stand it . . . unbearable.

''You were a teacher at Hunter College. Don't you remember?''

''AAArrrrgggghh!'' The scream was ripped out of him, and it didn't sound human.

''Parry!''

Parry pulled away from him and threw himself to the sidewalk, writhing. A terrible, terrible screaming kept issuing from his lips, as though he were being torn to pieces alive. As Jack watched, helpless, Parry curled up in a fetal position, his arms thrown over his head to protect himself. And screamed. And screamed.

The Red Knight came. He was here. His face was too hideous even to imagine, but fire was coming out of his helmet, fire was curling the edges of his beard, flames were streaming from his horse's nostrils, tongues of fire were burning along the shaft of his lance and springing hungrily from the razor-sharp head. The Red Knight's chain-mail armor was all ablaze, and sparks of fire exploded from the rim of his shield. He was here for Parry, because Parry must be destroyed. The Red Knight drew his sword, which also burned with streaks of fire. The war-horse's front hooves rose high in the air, twin powerful hammers to dash out Parry's brains.

Oh, God help me, thought Parry, cowering on the ground. This is the end. I'll never see the Holy Grail.

''Parry, are you all right?'' Jack knelt down beside him and held him by the shoulders. Parry opened his mouth to warn Jack away, but no words came out. Now the Red Knight would kill him, too. He shivered, waiting for the hooves to fall, for his brains to be crushed underfoot, for the cruel flaming sword to pierce his flesh, and for his heart's blood to flow along the shaft of the spear.

But it didn't happen. Nothing happened, and nobody died. After a minute Parry dared to open his eyes. The first thing he saw was Jack Lucas's face looking down at him, looking worried. And then he saw the Red Knight. The horse and rider were standing quite still, watching Parry and Jack, from about half a city block away. The horse shook his mane and moved restively, but he took a few steps back, not forward. The knight's mailed glove tightened on the reins. Parry stared in amazement. To him it seemed that horse and rider wanted to attack . . . but . . . *dared* not!

"Parry, answer me, are you all right?"

He turned his face to Jack, and it was joyous. "He knows who you are! I can tell! *We've got 'em! Come on!*"

And, before Jack could stop him, Parry had bounded to his feet and dashed out headlong into traffic, dodging some vehicles, being grazed by others. He ran down Fifth Avenue toward the Seventy-second Street entrance to Central Park, with taxi horns blaring at him and bus drivers cursing and shaking their fists.

"He's afraid!" he called back over his shoulder to Jack. "He's afraid of you! I can tell!"

"Oh, Jesus!" Jack breathed despairingly, and began to run after him. Everything was turning to shit; this was the last thing he wanted. Why the fuck didn't Parry just take the damn seventy dollars?

Parry saw the Red Knight wheel and turn, his horse's hooves pawing at the clouds. Horse and rider turned into the park with Parry running hell for leather after them. Parry's excitement made his feet fly.

Nothing like this had ever happened before. He had

the Red Knight on the run now, because Jack was the
One! Courage coursed through his knightly veins as
he gave chase. His legs pumped mightily. As he ran
through the park he could see the Red Knight ahead
of him—now in the bushes, now on a pathway. He
could hear the war steed's unshod feet thundering,
and the snort of air from its nostrils. The Red Knight
was fleeing. He was afraid, and for the first time Parry
was not afraid.

"Yes!" he cried in exaltation. "Yes!" Everywhere
the Red Knight galloped, Parry followed without tir-
ing. They raced through playgrounds, onto Frisbee
fields, through joggers and cyclists, past startled
mothers and nannies pushing strollers and carriages.
When the Red Knight tried to conceal himself, Parry
could see him plainly. At last they met.

On a high rock, silhouetted against the sky, horse
and rider stood at bay. A silence surrounded them.
Parry could see the war-horse's flanks heaving under
its heavy coat of mail, but he couldn't hear its ragged
breaths. He couldn't hear the strike of hooves against
stone or the clang of sword against shield. They were
isolated, horse and rider, encapsulated in stillness,
caught in the meshes of their own fear.

Parry had never experienced the Red Knight afraid.
His heart swelled to bursting with the wonder and the
joy of it, and a roaring battle cry escaped his lips,
shattering the protective silence. The horse reared,
the rider tugged at the reins, and the Red Knight
wheeled and disappeared, with Parry following at top
speed.

Jack Lucas's sides ached so much he couldn't take
another step. Yelling Parry's name, pleading for him
to stop, he'd chased that maniac little fucker over bike
path and jogger path, around water fountains, baby
carriages, and people walking their Jack Russells and
Shih Tzus on fancy leashes. Parry paid no attention,
but just kept running. The little bastard was fast, you

had to give him that, and it was obvious to Jack that he was convinced he was chasing somebody or something. Ten minutes into the chase, Jack lost sight of Parry, but he kept on running anyway.

Oh, God, Jack silently begged, just let this miserable day be over soon. Just let me survive this and I will never—repeat *never* butt into anybody else's business as long as I live. The path took a turn and Jack was faced by a large rock. Somehow he knew he had to climb it. His calf muscles screamed for mercy just at the thought of it. Boy, he'd no idea how out of shape a man could get without a Nautilus in only six months.

"Ohhhh . . . God . . . I'm dying," he moaned with his last panting breath. "I can't breathe, and I'm dying."

Reaching the top of the rock after enormous exertion, Jack was not surprised to find Parry sitting there, admiring the view of the Manhattan skyline as calmly as though he'd been sitting there on his ass all afternoon. Not a rasp in his breath or a drop of sweat on his brow. Jack wanted to kill him, the son of a bitch looked so goddamn blissful.

"Isn't this a beautiful spot, Jack?"

"Who have we been chasing!" Jack gasped through aching lungs. "Can I ask this question now?"

"He's gone now, but we had him on the run," Parry answered enthusiastically. "If we had horses, we would have had his ass! He's running scared."

"WHO? *Who's* running? Who have we been chasing?"

Parry looked at Jack, puzzled. "I thought you saw him," he said slowly.

Jack was so mad he was ready to detonate. "*Saw who?*"

"The Red Knight," Parry answered quietly.

"The Red . . . ?" Jack couldn't believe his ears. All this running and dodging, climbing and aching in every goddamn muscle, and there would be charley-horse hell to pay tomorrow, and all for a fucking *hallucination?*

That tore it. That was all. No more. Not ever. I hate this. Jack shook his head. "I gave you the money. You want to keep it, fine. You want to give it away, fine." He turned his plaintive gaze up to heaven. "I just want you to know that I gave him the money. Okay? Are we clear?"

"Who are you talking to, Jack?" Parry asked with real interest.

Before Jack could utter the swear word that sprang so readily to his lips, a desperate cry sounded in the distance.

"Do you hear that?" Parry asked eagerly, his whole face lighting up. "Oh, heaven be praised, in giving me an opportunity so soon of fulfilling the duties of my profession." He scrambled to his feet and struck a heroic pose. Jack groaned in dread.

"No! Leave me alone! Get away!" The voice was clearer now, although whether it was a man's or woman's was impossible to tell.

"These cries doubtless proceed from some miserable male or female who stands in need of my immediate aid and protection," Parry pronounced, and he was off and running in the direction of the voice, every cell of his being alive to his next chivalric adventure.

"This is too hard," Jack moaned. This fucking day was never, never going to end. Miserably, he trailed along after Parry.

Eleven

Parry pounded off in the direction of the cries, which had become more of a high, keening wail. Jack followed more slowly. "Over this way!" the high-pitched voice cried. "You're *missing* me! You should be *hitting* me!"

As the two approached the source of the wailing they could hear the neighing of horses and the sound of trotting hooves. A sudden bend in the road revealed a small, ragged man sitting in the center of the bridle path, blocking the way of the riders. Men and women on horseback took great pains to ride around him, but that only made the little guy more hysterical. When he saw Parry and Jack coming for him, the wailing grew in intensity until it was a hysterical scream.

"No! No! Get away, get *away!*"

Jack stopped circumspectly on the edge of the bridle path, but Parry darted directly onto the path and knelt down beside the man. "I'm not gonna hurt you," he soothed.

"That's what the other guy said," the small man wept. Somebody had evidently tried to rescue him earlier. "Please go away." The man had small, regular features and an enormous mustache that took up almost half his little face. On his head was a massive contusion, and it was bleeding.

"I want to help you," said Parry earnestly, examining the bump. There might be concussion.

"No, please, leave me alone."

"Come on now, you can't sit here. Let me help you up." Parry grabbed one arm and began tugging, but the little guy, who couldn't have weighed much more than a Great Dane, resisted furiously.

"*No!* I want a debutante on a horse to step on me! Leave me alone!"

Parry glanced around at the riders, most of them in jeans and shabby jackets, posting by on steeds rented by the hour from the Piedmont Stables over on West Eighty-third. "Sorry to tell you this, but the days of the debutantes are over."

At once, the man burst into tears of genuine grief. "Isn't that awful?" he sobbed. "Poor little Gloria. Poor Brenda Frazier. They ruined them! They ate them *alive!*"

"Parry," Jack called, itchy to leave. This little guy was obviously a couple of cards shy of a deck, with a few extra jokers thrown in. Even if Parry did succeed in hauling him to his feet, what the hell were they going to do with him afterward?

But Parry was already deeply caught up in his latest knightly deed, doing the so-called duties of his profession, and a knight must never allow himself to become distracted from the job at hand.

"Yeah, but what about Slim Keith? Or that little Guggenheim girl?" he asked very seriously. Parry took everything seriously, never passing judgment on the worth or the triviality of another's passions. But his attempt at consoling his new friend didn't appear to be working. He gave one more sharp tug, but the other man still resisted. Frail and emaciated though he was, that little gay guy was stronger than he looked. He made himself deadweight so he couldn't be moved.

"*Imposters!*" he sniffed. "Leave me alone!"

Parry kept on pulling, but to no avail. He just wasn't strong enough by himself to lift a man determined not to budge from the middle of a bridle path. "C'mon, Jack, lend a hand!" he called urgently.

Jack Lucas was far from eager to help. It wasn't so much picking this fellow up that bothered him, it was what might come later. They might get stuck with him. He already had one fruitcake on his hands; two fruitcakes were more than he wanted to deal with. "Listen," he said uncomfortably to Parry. "He just needs to sleep it off. Someone will take care of him."

"Who?" Parry snapped. "Mother Teresa? She's retired. C'mon, it's just us. Let's go!"

Jack shifted from foot to foot evasively. "Well, maybe he wants to stay here. Do . . . do you want to stay here?"

"Sure," the little man huffed. "I just love bleeding in horseshit. How very Gandhiesque of you."

He couldn't fight them both. Jack Lucas heaved a deep sigh and came over to take his other arm. Together, he and Parry managed to get him standing. As soon as he was on his feet the little guy with the big mustache uttered a tiny moan and passed out in Jack's arms.

The emergency room of a free city hospital is a scene out of hell. The ER at St. Alphonsus Hospital on Ninth Avenue made the homeless hangout under the Manhattan Bridge look like the Waldorf-Astoria. Jack Lucas's eyes went wide with horror; he could hardly believe what he was seeing. If the bridge was Dante and Gogol, the ER was Dante and Gogol playing Sartre's *No Exit* while rehearsing for *Marat/Sade*.

The large shabby anteroom was crowded with the wounded, looking ghastly under the harsh overhead lights. The benches, lined up against the institutional-green walls, were filled with them. Those who couldn't find seats stood lined up against the walls or squatted on the linoleum floor nearby.

Those who were too agitated to sit or stand still paced about endlessly, in search of something they would probably never find.

Some of the wounded exhibited physical injuries—a stab in the side that had bled through a man's shirt, turning it a cheerful shade of red. An older woman with a broken leg, crying in pain as she waited her turn to be called. A child who'd been bitten by a rat as he slept. A young woman, scarcely older than fifteen, with bruises all over her face and body where her boyfriend had kicked and beaten her.

Others were wounded just as seriously, but somewhat less visibly. These people bled on the inside. A drunk in delirium tremens, screaming horribly as snakes only he could see attacked him. A twelve-year-old junkie hooker coming down from an opiate high, scratching, scratching at her face and arms, begging for something to get her high again. Manic-depressives in the manic state, with a clear-crystal vision of aliens in spaceships. Manic-depressives in the depressive state, wanting only to die. Schizophrenics who were either catatonic and didn't move a muscle or who were hallucinating, their tortured bodies twitching and jerking uncontrollably. Some of them were confined in straitjackets, their arms strapped behind them.

None of these people had any money, or Blue Cross, or Medicare or other necessary social validation. All they had was their desperation, their will to survive. They were all in some kind of emergency, whether physical or mental or both. So they had congregated here, in this aptly named anteroom, bringing their emergencies with them, begging for attention. This place was truly a circus of the Bungled and the Botched. All it needed was the old philosopher Nietzsche as ringmaster. In the air, hovering over everything, was a miasma of harsh chemical odor—a mingling of antiseptic, urine, vomit, blood, iodine—that made it almost impossible to draw a breath. A line from Marlowe's *Faustus* came suddenly into Jack's mind. *Why, this is hell, nor am I out of it.*

The one common bond these people had, besides the fact that all of them were victims of one kind or another, was that they were all here waiting. Waiting to be helped. Waiting for somebody in authority, somebody with schooling and skill, to examine their wounds and suggest a cure. But where were the doctors? Jack realized suddenly that he'd seen no doctors since they'd brought Michael in. And almost no nurses.

From time to time a nurse came out and called a name. Once, twice, perhaps a third time. The name was never pronounced correctly, and it took a minute or so for its owner to recognize it and to shuffle or hobble or limp forward to a curtained cubicle where emergency care was presumably given and received. But it was a slow, tortuous process. Some of the people here had been waiting five hours or more. So what constituted an actual emergency? A nuclear holocaust?

Jack couldn't bring himself to actually enter the ER, but Parry dived right in. He half led, half carried Michael over to a bench that had just had a vacancy and parked him.

"Will you watch him for a minute, Jack?" he called.

There was nothing Jack wanted less than to walk into this room and baby-sit a half-starved derelict queen who identified with Brenda Diana Duff Frazier, the most celebrated society deb of half a century ago. The guy was filthy, bleeding, wore earrings, and he stank. Dragging his feet, Jack got his ass over to the bench, and before he could utter a protest, Parry dumped Michael into his arms and took off.

"Please, no," Michael sobbed. "I was born in a place like this. I don't wanna die here."

The person next to him got up from the bench, and Jack sat down next to Michael. What the hell was he supposed to do now? He looked around for Parry, but Parry was moving through the crowd like summer lightning, saying a big hello to everybody. He seemed to have a kind word for every man, woman, and child in the room, even for those who couldn't speak English. He took one old woman by the hands, looking deeply into her eyes, and it seemed to have a calming effect on her. He lifted a crying baby in his arms, and miraculously it stopped crying. Wherever he went, people seemed to feel a little better. Despite himself, Jack was impressed. Crazy he might be, but Parry knew how to make a difference in people's lives.

"I wanna go. . . ." Michael mumbled. "Just let me go. . . ."

"Uh, where do you want to go?" Jack asked.

"A real nice place I know about," Michael answered softly. "But we can't get there tonight."

"Well, maybe we can go there later."

Jack's answer only seemed to agitate Michael more. "No, no, we can't! We can't!"

Jack felt a sudden and most untypical stab of pity for the little fellow. "Come on," he said more gently. "Maybe we can. Where do you want to go?"

Michael sighed deeply. "Venice," he whispered. "Like Katharine Hepburn in *Summertime*." A sob escaped him, a cry of frustration and utter hopelessness. "Oh, why can't I be Katharine Hepburn?"

Jack stared at him, at a loss for words. He saw the homely thin face, the scraggly mustache, the bags under the eyes, the lines around the mouth of this aging homosexual mental case. Life's loser if ever there was one. A prime example of the grimness of the underclass. The Bungled and the Botched. A guy who had nothing at all going for him, no mojo, no luck.

And then a very strange thing happened to Jack Lucas. For the first time in years he made contact with another person, a contact that was real, not just a trade or a transaction.

He saw beneath the tired aging face to the soul within. Jack saw, not Michael the worn-out and discouraged little queen, but Michael the man, the human being, the person in need of solace and comfort. And, for the first time in his life, he felt the need to give some comfort to another. And he realized sadly that he didn't know how.

Parry knew how. Look at him now, handing out gobs of affection and comfort to every wounded person in the ER. Did that make Parry a better man than Jack? Jack Lucas had to admit that it probably . . . no, almost certainly, did.

"I wanna die," Michael wept. "I just wanna die." He laid his small head down on Jack's shoulder.

Jack felt his arm going around Michael's scrawny body, sort of awkwardly hugging him. He heard himself murmuring things like, "Hey, it's gonna be all right," meaningless comforting words he didn't really believe himself. And, while a little gay bum named Michael cried himself into exhaustion on Jack's muscular shoulder, much to his own astonishment, embarrassed as all hell, Jack Lucas just sat there and held him.

"That's it," sparkled Parry. "Okay, ready? Here we go." He raised up his arms. He sang the first line of the song about liking June in New York.

He cued a man in a straitjacket to give him the next line.

"I'm in the wrong place," muttered the schizophrenic.

"Aren't we all?" Parry chirped. Parry sang the second line himself. He waved his hand at the next crazy, who stared at him blankly, drooling a little.

Parry smiled encouragingly. He then sang the next line. And he pointed to a tattered and incredibly dirty bag lady whose swollen toes were peering out from her torn shoes.

"Where the hell am I gonna put the children?" shrieked the woman in her demented rage. "Goddamn daughter-in-law! Comes into my house looking for dust balls! Get the fuck outta my dining room, you asshole!"

"That's a wonderful feeling," Parry approved. "But you're stretching. Come on people . . . tempo, tempo. Allegro!" It was hard to get a good choral group going, especially when its members were locked up so tightly in their private hells, but Parry was always willing to give it a try. Sometimes the results surprised even him.

"Well, I'm a singer by trade," Michael was confiding to Jack in a breathy voice. "Summer stock . . . nightclub revues . . . that kind of thing. It used to be what I absolutely lived for! I can do every part of *Gypsy*, even backward," he added proudly. Then his voice dropped, and his face saddened. "But one night, in the middle of singing 'Funny,' it suddenly hit me. What does all this really mean?" He looked up into Jack's face for corroboration, and a surprised Jack discovered that he knew exactly what Michael was driving at. When you came right down to it, what the hell did it all really mean?

"That, plus the fact that I watched all my friends die," Michael added, subdued. "God, I sound like a veteran. My dad would be so proud of me!" He giggled, and felt much better. Felt pretty good, in fact.

"Pizza!" A pizza delivery boy appeared in the

doorway of the ER, carrying six or seven stacked boxes. Instantly, he was surrounded by a swarm of doctors and nurses, waving money. Son of a bitch, Jack thought, so there are doctors in this hospital after all! Where the fuck have they been hiding?

"Jack, it's after four." Parry turned up suddenly, and his usually cheery face looked anxious. "We're going to be late. We're going to miss her if we don't go now." He was getting pretty agitated, like his pants were full of insects.

Jack stood up, his shoulders drooping in exhaustion. He looked down at the fragile Michael. "Uh, I've got to run. I've been doing this all day. Are you going to be all right?"

Michael waved one thin hand in a grande dame gesture. "Oh, please! I was born a Catholic in Brooklyn. I've been to hell and back. I'll be fine." He smiled self-consciously at Jack. "Thanks," he said with sincerity. "You're a gem."

Jack smiled back just as self-consciously. Nobody had ever called him a gem before, and he kind of liked it.

Jack Lucas couldn't remember ever having been this tired. He'd had a long day, a full day, an unreal day. Life in the fast lane. In the last six or so hours, he'd traversed most of Manhattan. First, all the way to the bottom of the island, to the Manhattan Bridge. Then north by northwest to Twenty-fourth Street. Next an uptown trek to Seventy-fourth and Fifth, followed by an excursion into Central Park at sixty miles per hour in hot pursuit of a mythical invisible enemy. Then a delightful sojourn into the bowels of a city hospital emergency room. And now, with the ebullient Parry acting as tour guide, Jack was standing in the center of the grand concourse at Grand Central Station, crossroads of a million private lives, gigantic stage on which are played a thousand dramas daily.

All he needed were a pair of Gucci loafers, a Rolex watch, a navy-blue suit, a white shirt with pens in the pocket, a striped necktie, and an auto-reflex talking camera and he could be a Japanese tourist. What did Parry have in mind next? A little swim through the Narrows to Staten Island? A hike up to the Cloisters? Parry not only liked New York in June, but in January, November, April, and August.

They had arrived at Grand Central virtually on the run, to look for the delicious darling of Parry's loving heart, to seek out one small, skinny figure among the thousands of massed commuter bodies that pulsated across the concourse floor at this evening rush hour, human lemmings rushing pell-mell toward the sea of homebound trains.

Jack surveyed the mob scene with some dismay. "We're never gonna find her in this crowd," he told Parry.

Parry smiled confidently. The hands of the large terminal clock showed three minutes to five. "She's like clockwork," he assured Jack. "She's always on time, every day." Then his face fell. "She's late!" His bright blue eyes began to scan the crowd with anxiety.

Jack had never been in Grand Central Station except on his way to somewhere else, taking a train to a Connecticut weekend, for example, or to some rich friend's fancy renovated farmhouse in upstate New York. He'd always get a reserved seat in the parlor car, the one with comfortable chairs and bar service. Now he wasn't going anywhere, thanks to Parry. He had leisure to look around him.

Jack was interested to see that the station had a flora and fauna of its own, an ecosystem apart from the rushing commuters. A large homeless community had taken up residence here. Jack Lucas read the papers; he knew that from time to time the police cracked down on the station, rounding up the homeless and dragging them off to shelters. "Cleaning up Grand Central," they called it. But these were people, not dirt. You can't run an Electrolux over human beings. Besides, the homeless kept coming back. Where else did they have to go at night? In the station they could keep warm and try to eke out a living from begging for money.

Beggars and panhandlers were all over the station; they seemed to have staked out fixed territories, respecting one another's turf. The difference between them was that the panhandlers would accost their marks, asking for money, sometimes even demanding it. The beggars tended to stay in one place and call out to passersby, usually because the beggars were missing at least one limb and couldn't get around that easily. Parry appeared to know them all by name; now, why wasn't Jack surprised to learn that?

They were standing between the ticket windows and the information booth, where Parry could keep one eye on the terminal clock and the other on the pedestrian traffic to catch the first sight of his lady fair. A few feet away, a legless Vietnam vet named Sid sat in a wheelchair, a Styrofoam cup held out in his hand. Every now and then, somebody would drop a coin in the cup and hurry on by without making eye contact.

"God bless you! Have a safe trip home!" Sid would call out, not meaning a word of it. "Ya hear that Jimmy Nickels got picked up yesterday?" he asked Parry. But Parry was too busy searching the passing faces for the only lovely one of his fantasies, and Jack alone was left to answer him.

"Oh, yeah?" He hadn't the foggiest who Jimmy Nickels was, but he was willing enough to make conversation.

"He got caught pissin' on a bookstore. The man's a pig. Thank you, babe, God bless you. Safe trip. There's no excuse for that. We're heading for social anarchy when people start pissing on bookstores."

The man had a unique point of view, and Jack couldn't help but smile. He turned to share it with

Parry, but Parry was all a-tremble, looking like one of those nervous dogs that people tie to street lamps when they go inside to shop. He was starting to pace, three steps this way, three steps back. Four steps that way, four steps back. His eyes were bright with worry, and his brow wrinkled.

"You'll never see her in this crowd," Jack told Parry again, but the little man just shook his head anxiously and kept looking.

A commuter pitched a coin in the direction of Sid's cup, missing it. The quarter hit the floor and began to roll away. Sid bent to retrieve it, but he had no balance, and Jack chased after the coin and brought it back for him.

"The asshole!" he scowled. "The guy didn't even look at you." It didn't occur to him that this was an ironic observation coming from a man who not that long ago wouldn't bother to roll down a limousine window to give a beggar a coin, because "a couple of quarters wouldn't make any difference." Jack Lucas was beginning to change, but the depth and extent of the changes hadn't yet begun to sink in.

"He's paying so he doesn't have to look at me." Sid grinned sardonically. "What he doesn't know is that I'm providing a service for him. Guy goes to a job every day for eight hours, seven days a week, he gets his nuts caught so tight in a vise, he gets to questioning the very fabric of his existence. But one day, about quitting time, his boss says, 'Bob, come into my office and kiss my ass for me.' And Bob is going to think, 'The hell with it. I don't care what happens. I just want to see the expression on his face when I jab this pair of scissors into his arm.' "

Parry was pacing really rapidly now, his eyes darting nervously from the crowd to the hands of the clock: 5:01 . . . 5:02. His world was beginning to fall apart.

"But then he thinks of me," Sid continued. "He

says to himself, 'Wait a minute! At least I got two arms and two legs and I ain't begging for a living. Sure enough, he puts down the scissors and puckers right up.''

Jack laughed appreciatively; this was some philosopher. Old Friedrich Nietzsche had nothing on Sid.

"I'm what you call a moral traffic light. Like I'm saying, *'Red!* Go no further.' ''

There was a small gasp from Parry, and Jack turned his head. Moving awkwardly, pushing with her elbows through the crowd that pitched and tossed against her, was the girl from the Haggensen Building. At once, Parry moved off in pursuit, keeping a distance of about five feet between them. He was perfectly happy now, because after minutes of anxiety that felt like hours, his life was back on schedule. He had the most beautiful woman in the world in sight, and Grand Central Station must be the most magical structure in the world, more beautiful even than Versailles or the Taj Mahal. Everything was perfect. Parry heard the sound of train whistles as a Strauss waltz and saw the pushing and shoving of the commuters as a graceful ballet.

The girl reached her Metro North platform and vanished into a train. Parry stood on the platform in an ecstasy until the train pulled out and dived down into the tunnel. As Jack came up beside him he was watching the last car of the train go around the bend in the tunnel.

"God," Parry breathed. "Just one night with her. I'd die happy."

Yes! said Jack Lucas to himself, with a lifting of his heart. He could hear the albatross stirring back to life, he could feel its wings move, just a little.

Twelve

If Jack Lucas didn't have a spare moment during this hectic, manic day to give a thought to Anne Napolitano waiting back home for him, Anne certainly had plenty of time to think about Jack. He'd left the house early in the morning without telling her one word about where he was going, or who he was going to be with, or when he'd be back. So, naturally, when he didn't show up, first she suspected the worst, then, hours later, when she'd been waiting for him all day and part of the night, she was sure of the worst. No matter how vehemently he denied it, Jack must be seeing another woman.

For eight long hours Anne worked in the store renting videotapes while her mind ran a videotape of Jack with somebody else. Although she didn't want to, she couldn't help imagining him making love to another woman—blond, no doubt, and skinny, without tits. Her emotions veered between misery and rage, and her rage ranged between fury at the two-timer and fury at herself for letting him get away with it, and for caring about him in the first place.

At six o'clock Anne locked the door of the Video Spot, pulled down the iron night gates, and went upstairs to her apartment. Because she was so nervous, she went into her tiny kitchen and used up a lot of negative energy pounding and breading veal cutlets. She could pretend that the cutlets were Jack.

Then she spent another full hour preparing an enormous pan of lasagna with meat sauce. Why she was standing on her feet in a hot kitchen cooking Jack Lucas's favorite foods while the bastard was out doing the two-time two-step was beyond her, but the mere thought of it furnished fresh fuel for Anne's anger.

Dinner was on the table at eight, but no word from Jack. Anne sat down to a solitary meal, but managed only to push the food from side to side on her plate without actually tasting any. By nine o'clock, the cutlets were soggy and cold, and the lasagna was congealed rubber in the pan. And still not even a phone call.

"I do not need this!" she said out loud through gritted teeth as she carried the uneaten food from the dining area back to the kitchen. "A woman my age! There's a person in here!" For one moment she contemplated throwing the food into the garbage, but Anne had been raised poor in a house where food was sacred, so she got out the plastic wrap and let the gesture go.

"You come! You go!" she shouted at the imaginary Jack as she scrubbed out the encrusted baking pan. "And all I do is cook like a jerk! You're a waste of good lasagna. I don't need this! Find yourself another dope!" With trembling fingers, Anne lit a cigarette and sank down at the dining-room table, her face in her hands.

"You son of a bitch," she growled at invisible Jack, and then fell silent. They say ventilating your anger, letting it out, makes you feel better. But Anne Napolitano didn't feel any better. In fact she felt rotten, because she knew she was trapped. Trapped by her own emotions. No matter what she said, or how loudly she hollered, Anne still loved the miserable cheating bastard. Stubbing out the smoke, she burst into tears.

Meanwhile, the object of her wrath actually wanted nothing more than to be home scarfing down a good hot Italian meal. He was worn out from a very long day of playing reluctant tail to Parry's manic kite. Darkness had fallen, and here the two of them were still roaming around, a mad Don Quixote and his reluctant Sancho Panza.

They had fetched up at last on the Sheep Meadow in Central Park, a lovely vast lea where sheep really had grazed until the meat shortage during the Second World War had put an end to them. During the day, kids smoked pot and threw Frisbees to their mutts on the Sheep Meadow, mothers put their babies down on the grass to toddle, and old folks took walks here with slow, careful steps. But at night Sheep Meadow was a dark and deserted expanse that could be home or hiding place to almost anything.

"Don't you think it's time to go now?" Jack demanded anxiously. "Running around here during the day is one thing, but at night we could be killed by a wide variety of people."

"Well, that's just stupid," Parry retorted. He wasn't tired at all, although Jack was about ready to drop where he stood. "This is my park just as much as it is theirs. You think it's fair for them to keep us out just because they think we might get killed or something?"

"Yes, I think it's very fair," said Jack, and he meant it.

"Well, I don't."

Jack fished his pack of cigarettes out of his pocket and lit one. It took a few seconds because the night breeze kept blowing out the match. When at last it was lit, and he looked up, he saw an astounding sight. Parry was half-naked, his shirt and outer garments strewn on the grass, and he was in the act of zipping down his pants.

"What are you doing?" Jack gasped, horrified.

"I'm cloudbusting, Jack," Parry answered matter-of-factly. "Have you ever done any cloudbusting? You lie on your back and you concentrate on the clouds, and you break them apart with your mind. It's wild!"

The pants were off now, down around his ankles, and Parry was hopping around to kick them away. He wore no underwear. His muscular little hairy body was completely naked. "But you have to be nude," he continued. "Otherwise, you can't diffuse the psychic energy." Naked, he lay down on the grass in full view of the moon, his head pillowed on his arms, completely at home.

"You can't do this!" a shocked Jack Lucas exclaimed. "This is New York! Nobody lies naked in a field in New York. It's too . . . midwestern!"

Parry got up and danced around laughing. "Wild! It's really freeing! Come on and try it, Jack. You feel the air on your body . . . your nipples are hard . . . your little guy's dangling in the wind. Everybody in the city is busy with their business and no one knows we're bare-assed in the middle of it. Come on!"

"You're pissin' me off, Parry," Jack warned.

But Parry was too caught up in his Dionysian revelry to pay attention. He kept dancing around Jack, yelling, "Free yourself! Free yourself!" Jack kept glancing about nervously. He couldn't decide which would be more welcome now—the sight of the cops or the muggers. This was the stupidest thing that nut case had pulled yet, and Jack Lucas was damned if he was going to let himself be dragged into it.

"C'mon, Jack!" Parry's exuberance was escalating as his dancing became even more frenzied. He resembled some prehistoric savage in the throes of a religious ritual. "Do you know why you should do it? 'Cause it feels good!"

"*No!* I'm not doing that!"

"Yes! Yo! Get back to your roots! C'mon, Jack, free up the little guy and let it flap in the breeze!" And, throwing back his head, Parry began to yip and howl like a wild dog.

Of all the embarrassing stunts Parry had pulled today, this was by far the looniest. "I'm not doing this!" Jack yelled at Parry. "This is nuts! This is too nuts! I'm leaving! I mean it!"

He walked away a few feet and then turned to look back. Parry was on the ground again, lying on his back in the grass with his arms tucked under his head, staring blissfully up at the moon. With a snort of anger, Jack kept walking.

"Huh, little guy," he muttered scornfully to himself. "I mean, the man talks to invisible people. He sees invisible horses, and he's lying naked in the middle of Central Park. I should be surprised? I'm not surprised. I'm fuckin' outta my mind to even be here!"

Parry raised himself up on one elbow. "Who are you talking to, Jack?" he asked amiably.

"I'm talking to the Little People," Jack snarled back.

"Are they here?" Parry sat up, excited.

"Yes! They're saying, 'Jack, get thee to the nearest liquor store and buy thyself a fifth of Jack Daniel's, that ye may be shit-faced.' "

"They said that?"

Jack turned back, completely out of patience, and yelled at Parry. "You're out of your fuckin' mind!"

"Bingo," Parry said triumphantly.

Christ, whaddya gonna do? With a sigh of frustration, Jack walked back and lay down beside Parry, fully clothed. He stared up into the night sky and the moon shining golden on the clouds. Long moments passed.

"They're not moving," he said at last.

"Concentrate," Parry advised. Jack undid the top

two buttons on his shirt, as a compromise to nudity-in-cloudbusting. Maybe it helped a little. From time to time a wisp of cloud would drift across the face of the moon, but the large masses of cloud formations appeared to be slumbering in the sky.

It was, as Parry said, a beautiful evening, calm and still. To Jack, it was . . . almost . . . pleasant to lie here in the grass beside Parry. The moonlight bathed them both in its radiance and it was a relief to have Parry at rest for once. Jack had never seen Parry when he wasn't darting about like a hungry hummingbird.

"What if some homophobic jogger runs by and kills us to get back at his father?" Jack wondered half to himself.

" 'Jack Lucas Found Dead . . . Beside a Dead Naked Man . . . The Two Were Dead . . . His Companion Was Naked.' "

Jack recited the imaginary headlines, musing out loud. "I hate it when they use the word 'companion,' it's so insinuating. Although, it would probably boost the sales of my biography. The public has a fascination with celebrity murders that involve nakedness." He added bitterly, "Bastards."

"I may be going out on a limb here," Parry remarked, "but you don't seem like a happy camper."

Jack only grunted in reply.

"Did you ever hear the story of the Fisher King?" Parry asked suddenly.

"No."

Parry began to speak very quietly, as though telling the tale to a child to make him sleep.

"It begins with the Fisher King as a boy—who had to spend a night alone in the forest so that he could become a king. While he was alone in the forest, he was visited by a sacred vision. Out of the fire appeared the Holy Grail, the symbol of God's divine grace. And a voice spoke to the boy, saying,

'You shall be the keeper of the Grail, that it may heal the hearts of men.' But the boy was blinded by greater visions, by a life ahead filled with power and glory . . . and beauty. . . . And in this state of radical amazement, he felt . . . for a brief moment . . . not like a boy, but invincible, like God.

"And so he reached into the fire to take the Grail. And the Grail vanished. And the boy's hands were left in the flames, to be terribly wounded. Now, as this boy grew older, his wound grew deeper, until one day, he had no faith left in any man, not even himself. He couldn't love or feel love. And he was so sick with experience that he started to die. As he did, so did his kingdom, and that terrified his people, so they mobilized to find the one thing they knew could save him, the Holy Grail.''

Jack Lucas found himself completely caught up in the story, and in the magical eloquent way that Parry recited it in the moonlight. This must have been what it was like when he was sane, he thought bitterly. Henry Sagan must have been a wonderful teacher, in love with his material and able to transmit the beauty and wonder of it into young minds. A pang of regret nibbled at his heart as Jack realized that he would never know the man Henry Sagan, and that he wanted to, very much. He had a sudden sense of grief and loss.

"One day," Parry went on, "a fool wandered into the castle and found the king alone. Being simple-minded, he didn't see a king, he saw a man alone and in pain.

'' 'What ails you, friend?' he asked the king. The king replied, 'I'm thirsty. I need a sip of water to cool my throat.' So the fool took a cup from the bedside table, filled it with water, and handed it to the king. As the king began to drink he realized that his wound was healed. He looked at his hands, and there in them was that which he had sought all his life, the Holy Grail. And he turned to the fool and asked, 'How could you find what my brightest and bravest could not?'

"And the fool replied, 'I don't know. I only knew that you were thirsty.' "

The story of the Fisher King came to an end; Parry fell silent. Jack wanted to say something, but he was at a loss for words.

"Very beautiful, isn't it?" said Parry in a half whisper, and Jack nodded.

"I think I heard it at a lecture once . . . I don't know . . . a professor . . . at Hunter—" Parry broke off, confused and disoriented and suddenly frightened.

Jack turned to look at him. The small man was trembling. "Parry, Parry, hey . . ."

"What was I saying?" Parry asked, a look of panic on his face. He was staring straight ahead, and Jack turned to see what he was staring at. There was nothing.

But it wasn't nothing. Jack didn't see the Red Knight, but Parry did. He was sitting on his warhorse only about thirty feet away, watching. His sword was drawn; his lance rested across the horse's back. And Parry knew what the Red Knight was thinking. He was thinking, Soon, Parry, soon. You won't always have Jack around to protect you. Someday soon, I'll come upon you alone. And when I do . . ." A shaft of moonlight glinted off the deadly sword, and Parry shuddered in fear.

Picking up Parry's tattered jacket, Jack wrapped it around the small shivering figure. Parry laid his head back down on the grass, but Jack could sense his continued uneasiness.

"How come you never asked that girl for a date?" he asked, to change the subject.

Parry sat up and took a cautious look. The Red Knight had disappeared. He caught his breath in relief. "I can't *ask* her. I have to *earn* her," he explained, in a tone that implied that Jack ought to know better.

"It's the twentieth century, Parry, you don't have to earn a woman."

Parry nodded doubtfully. "Maybe, after we get the Grail . . ."

Jack's heart sank. "We"? Where the hell did he keep getting "we"?

"Well, see, she can help you get the Grail," he said hastily, trying to recollect what little he knew about the Middle Ages. "Women are great . . . they make homes . . . and they . . . y'know . . . they kill the livestock so the knights can go out and get Grails and . . . slaughter villages with a clear head. I mean, where would Arthur be without Guinevere?"

"Happily married, probably," Parry answered.

Oh, yeah, right, Jack had forgotten how *that* legend had turned out. "Well, that's a bad example. But trust me on this. A woman who loves you keeps you going . . . gives you strength . . . makes you feel like you can do anything."

"Is that what your girlfriend does for you?" Parry asked eagerly.

The question caught Jack by surprise and threw him off balance. Suddenly he thought of Anne and felt guilty. How *did* he feel about Anne Napolitano? He pushed the question out of his mind, unable to deal with it.

"Sure," he lied.

Jack woke up stiff as a board and shivering with cold. The ground was icy and rocky and damp; he couldn't believe he'd actually slept right here for hours. He brought his wrist up to his face and made himself focus on his watch. It was early, not much after eight in the morning, but already the joggers were skittering through Central Park in all directions, like cockroaches when you turn on the kitchen lights.

Why was he sleeping in the park? He hadn't even been drinking. Oh, yeah, cloudbusting. Jack looked over to where Parry had been sleeping, but the little man was gone. Thank God, his scattered clothing was gone, too, so Jack had some grounds for hope that Parry had dressed himself before he took off. Probably didn't want to wake him.

He suddenly flashed on where Parry must be. It was a weekday, Thursday. Parry had to be in front of the Haagensen Building, waiting for the girl of his dreams to show up for work. Right. Jack stood up a little shakily, every muscle protesting, and brushed himself off. Then he walked over to Fifth Avenue, pushed his way onto a crowded downtown bus, and got off a block after the Haagensen Building. He walked back, careful not to let Parry, whom Jack spotted at his customary station, see him coming. Parry was so focused on the revolving doors that he never noticed Jack slipping into the side entrance of the building.

Taking up his station near the elevators, Jack looked at his watch again. Three minutes to nine. If the girl was as predictable in her habits as Parry claimed she was, she'd be here . . . right . . . about now! And there she was, clumsily pushing her way through the nine o'clock crowd of workers to get to her elevator.

Jack maneuvered himself behind her and got into the same elevator. He turned his face away so that she couldn't make out his features, but he needn't have bothered. The young woman was oblivious of everything and everybody, not looking at anybody else in the elevator, but keeping her eyes to the front, waiting for her floor to come up.

Seen up close, the girl Parry was so enchanted by had pure, beautiful skin and fine large eyes, although

the rest of her could really stand one of those magazine beauty makeovers. She got off at the eighth
floor, and so did Jack. When she turned the corner
down the corridor, Jack hung behind, not wishing to
be seen following, but he kept his eye on her as she
went through a pair of glass doors to an office.

After she went inside, Jack moved forward and
looked at the office doors. Printed on them in gold
and black lettering was TWO HEARTS PUBLISHING,
INC. Jack waited a moment, straightening his rum-
pled jacket and brushing at his unruly hair with the
palms of his hands, then he pushed the office door
open and went inside.

He found himself in a reception area decorated by
a couple of dusty couches, a table with an ashtray,
and a reception desk. On the walls were framed paperback covers, presumably from Two Hearts Publishing's own list. They were all romances—busty
young women in low-cut gowns shrinking away while
handsome men wearing shirts with long, flowing
sleeves bent lustfully over them, one hand on the
girl's bodice and the other on a pistol or a sword. If
Parry's lady loved reading this garbage, she was certainly working in the right place.

"Yes?" A crisp voice from the reception desk
challenged him. A mildly attractive girl with a fluffy
perm and too much lipstick was glaring at Jack as
though he'd come in on the bottom of her shoe.

He knew he looked like a bum. What did she expect? He'd been out all day and all night, running
himself ragged around the city, and he hadn't had a
chance to shave or bathe. He desperately needed a
change of clothes, a toothbrush, and a comb. No
receptionist worth her paycheck would let him get a
foot in the door. Jack knew that.

But Jack Lucas had a secret weapon. He had
charm. He knew he was good-looking, with thick
hair, a good body, attractive blue eyes, a great grin

and deep dimples, but the big armament, the nuclear warhead, was his infallible ability to turn on the charm. Charm, don't fail me now!

"Could you help me?" he asked sweetly, looking into the receptionist's eyes and letting charm flow out of him like syrup on an Eggo. "What was the name of that girl who just came in?"

Girl? "What girl? I didn't notice," the receptionist said, caught in Jack Lucas's blue-eyed stare like a fish in a net.

How to describe her? "Uh, she was wearing a kind of, that is, a plain . . . she isn't pretty . . . her hair looks like . . ." He made strings of his fingers to indicate stringy hair.

"Oh, Lydia!"

Lydia. Good. He had a first name, and that was a start. "Lydia what?"

The girl fluffed out her curls, to show Jack what real hair should look like. "God, I have no idea. She's worked here for fifteen years and I have no idea. I'll call her."

"No!" Jack said quickly. "No, no, that's all right. I thought I knew her . . . but thanks." Rewarding the receptionist with one of his biggest smiles, he got out of there.

Parry was not on the street when Jack emerged from the side entrance. He felt kind of good. He had a name—Lydia—and a venue—Two Hearts Publishing. Now all he needed was a plan.

Thirteen

Anne was busy writing up an order for a videotape rental when she was certain she heard footsteps in her apartment above the store. That bastard Jack must be home. Twenty-four hours late, but home.

As soon as she could, she ducked out of the Video Spot and ran upstairs. She found Jack Lucas sitting on her sofa, the Yellow Pages open on his lap. He looked like hell, scruffy and none too clean, like somebody who'd been sleeping in Central Park all night. When Anne came into the room, Jack was saying into the phone, "Yes, is this Two Hearts Publishing? May I speak to Lydia, please?"

Anne could hardly believe her ears. The nerve of the bum! "Lydia?" He was calling some bimbette! And on her phone bill, too!

She approached him menacingly, claws out, ready to kill, but Jack wasn't even paying attention. This irritated Anne even more. Fire flashed out of her black eyes, her breasts heaved in anger, and the very curls in her black hair were electric with indignation.

"You are calling *Lydia?* From my apartment you are calling *Lydia?*" she demanded.

"Hello, I'd like to speak to Lydia." Jack had gotten through to the right department.

"Lydia? Lydia who!" Anne reached angrily for the phone, but Jack held it out of her reach.

He put his hand over the mouthpiece. "I don't

know her last name,'' he said. ''I'll be off in a minute.''

Some tramp without even a last name? This was the final straw for Anne, and she let her temper fly. Furiously, she began punching at Jack, hitting him in the neck, on the shoulder, wherever she could reach, while he fended her off with his elbows and continued to cling to the phone.

''Son of a *bitch!*'' she yelled. ''You stay out all night, I don't even get a friggin' phone call!''

''Ow! Don't! Quit it!'' Then he spoke into the phone. ''What? No, I don't know her last name . . . her name is Lydia. Can I speak to her?''

But Anne was far from ready to quit it. ''You stroll in here at noon, without a stinkin' word. I got two people out sick. You think I need this?! I . . . do . . . not . . . *need* . . . this!'' Another hefty wallop, this time a lucky punch, connected hard with Jack's ear.

''Forget it!'' Jack hollered into the phone. ''Goodbye!'' He slammed down the receiver and gave Anne his full attention. He was aware that he owed her a decent explanation, but how could he explain Parry and Parry's bizarre obsessions? Or the crazy idea that Jack himself had come up with?

''I was not with a woman last night,'' he said quietly. ''I was with Parry.''

Anne's eyes widened in surprise. ''The moron?''

''He's not a moron,'' said Jack emphatically.

''And who's Lydia?'' Anne didn't let go easily.

''Lydia is the girl Parry likes. And I thought, if I could get them together, I . . .''

''What?'' Anne demanded. ''The curse will be lifted? Gimme a break, puh-leeze!'' Her lively face registered scornful disbelief.

Jack fumbled to find the right words. ''I . . . uh . . . you're not going to understand this—''

"Don't treat me like I'm stupid," snapped Anne. "It pisses me off."

Jack nodded; fair enough. "Sorry . . . you're right. It's just that . . . I feel . . . indebted to him. I thought, well, if I could only help him in some way, you know? Get him this girl he loves? Then . . . maybe . . . things might change for me, too. My luck, you know . . . maybe it could . . . ahhhh, forget it! It's just a dumb fuckin' idea."

Anne regarded him thoughtfully. The last vestige of suspicion still clung like crumbs to the corners of her mind. But consider. Jack was sober, for a change; he appeared to be sincere, and God knows his luck had been terrible. Now the crumbs of suspicion dissolved, and she felt suddenly guilty for having doubted him. Poor schmuck, she'd been so hard on him. Just look at his disappointed face.

"Aww, you big galoot," she said affectionately. "You're such a mess. Well, listen, stranger things have been known to happen. Here, let me do it. What's the name of the place and the phone number?"

Jack dialed the number and handed Anne the telephone. "Hello," she said crisply, "Is that Two Hearts Publishing? Good. This is Mr. Jack Lucas's secretary. Mr. Lucas is attempting to reach one of your employees, a Miss Lydia—wait, let me check my notes. Oh, Sinclair? Lydia Sinclair? Yes, I believe that's the person. Put her on, please."

Grinning, she handed the phone over to Jack, who threw her a grateful and admiring look. When she had a mind to, Anne could be really something.

A woman's voice came on the line. "Hello?"

"Hello, Lydia?"

"Yes, who is this, please?" Her voice surprised Jack. It was not the timid squeak of the mousy little wimp she appeared to be, but a rather loud, abrasive bray.

"This is Jack Lucas," he said in his best radio-announcer voice, "and I'm calling from Video Spot video rentals."

"Yes?" The voice sounded suspicious, as though Lydia Sinclair were going to hang up on the caller if he didn't make his point soon.

Jack thought fast, coming up with a ploy. "Yes, well, you are a credit-card holder, aren't you?" *Please, please, let her be a credit-card holder.*

"Yes, so?" challenged Lydia.

Jack sighed silently in relief. "Well, Lydia, I have some good news for you. Congratulations. Out of several thousand card holders, in conjunction with major credit-card companies—"

"Which ones?" Lydia demanded.

Which ones? What kind of a question was that? "Uh . . . all of them. Which means *you* have just won a free membership at our store on Eighth Avenue!" He pushed the play button on his tape recorder and happy circus music poured into the receiver and out into Lydia Sinclair's ear.

"How did this happen?" Lydia asked brusquely when the music stopped. She sounded definitely suspicious, as though he were trying to sell her something. Which, of course, he was, although she'd probably keel over in a dead faint if she could actually see who it was he was selling. Lydia and Parry, now *there* was an odd couple!

"Your name was picked."

There was a pause on the line, and then Lydia's voice returned, sounding somewhat confused. "Uh, picked? I don't . . . I don't understand. Was I on a list? Did you pick my name off a list or was it out of a hat or something?"

"A list." This was like pulling teeth. Jack was starting to sweat.

"I . . . uh . . . what's going on? Were there a lot of people in the room or just you or what?"

God, this woman was so literal-minded that getting through to her was like ramming a stone wall! Didn't she have any imagination? "Well, there was . . . what's the difference?" Jack asked, beginning to run out of patience.

Lydia began to stammer nervously. "Well . . . I mean . . . I don't know you . . . I don't . . . I never . . . I've never won anything in my life . . . and I don't even have a VCR."

"You get a free VCR with membership!" Jack announced, then Anne punched him really hard in the arm. "Uh . . . for a short time, until you get your own," he amended. "Listen, why don't you just come down to the store and you can check it out. See if you're interested."

"Did Phyllis tell you to call me?" Lydia asked paranoically. "Did Phyllis in Accounting tell you to call me? This is a joke, right?"

"No!" Jack yelled in frustration. *"I told you! You won a contest!"*

There was a click in his ear. Lydia Sinclair had hung up the phone.

Turning to Anne, who was grinning and shaking her head, Jack moaned. "This is going to be rough. Oh, Jesus, is this going to be rough."

The plot that Jack finally devised out of desperation was so absurd that it would have been laughable except for one thing. He himself was the fool who was going to have to see that it was pulled off correctly. Anne went to the store to have the balloons printed, and Jack, cursing his fate, cursing Lydia, cursing Parry, cursing life, went in search of Michael, the gay little crazy he'd last seen in the emergency room at St. Alphonsus.

Strangely enough, Jack located Michael before Anne had finished ordering the balloons. There seemed to be a kind of bum underground, a network of the homeless, and somehow Jack had become, thanks to Parry, a recognizable member of it. With the information he was given, he found Michael not ten blocks away from the Video Spot, cruising Eighth Avenue. By the time Jack had finished explaining his plan, Michael was ecstatic.

"I'll do it. Of course I'll do it. I'd do anything for you, Jack. You're my friend. Besides, it sounds like the funnest thing!"

Funnest for you, maybe, Jack thought as he rode up in the elevator with Michael next to him. But not for me. Michael had rung in some embellishments to the plan, one or two unexpected ruffles and flourishes. Like full drag, for example.

Jack's eyes had popped out of his head when the little man turned up at the Haagensen Building wearing a costume that could only be described as grotesque outrageous—all spangles and flirty hems and off-the-shoulder see-through, plus high heels. It was topped by a wig and a big picture hat, from under which Michael's tiny face appeared in theatrical makeup—eyelashes mascaraed, cheeks rouged, lips a bright red, and that large mustache sitting smack in the middle of everything. When he saw him coming, Jack wanted to turn and run and hide.

Well, it was too late to do anything about it now. Jack shoved the bright yellow balloons into Michael's hands. Anne had had them printed up with "Video Spot," and the store's address and phone number. She'd instructed Jack specifically not to lose them, because they just might come in handy at the store. Two or three more were printed with "Congratulations, Lydia!" and these Anne didn't particularly want to see again.

Together, Jack and Michael rode up to the eighth floor. Thank God there was nobody else in the elevator, because Michael was warming up, getting into the spirit of things by humming and camping and fluffing up his ruffles. Jack stared at the ceiling and hoped fervently that nobody would get on the elevator between the ground floor and the eighth. That was all he needed, for them to be caught in this together by somebody from the real world.

A little hand touched his arm, and a voice sobbed, "I'm Anne Morrow Lindbergh, and I can't find my baby!"

Jack looked down, startled, at Michael, who was dabbing at his eyes with a lace hankie. Despite himself, Jack had to laugh.

"See." Michael grinned. "I knew I could make you smile."

The elevator came to a stop on eight and the doors opened. "Listen," Jack said warningly, "one chorus and out! Got it?"

"I'm a man with a mission, Jack." Clutching the balloons, Michael flounced out and down the hall, his high heels clacking on the vinyl flooring.

Jack shook his head. "I can't believe I'm on a first-name basis with these people," he mumbled to himself as the elevator carried him back down to the lobby.

In less than the space of a week, Jack Lucas had gone from a black, boozy, shitty, depressing, morally reprehensible but relatively normal existence into the Twilight Zone. Crazies were now his bosom buddies and boon companions. One of them, a man who hadn't worn out a pair of shoes since 1964, thought he was Ethel Merman, while the other, who was fixated on the homliest girl in New York, heard fat little fairies telling him to find the Holy Grail. Bums had become Jack's familiars, they recognized him on the street and hailed him as a brother. How the fuck had he gotten himself into this mess? Oh, right, he remembered. All he'd tried to do was kill himself. Was that such a crime?

Upstairs, Michael and his yellow balloons went wafting down the corridor and in through the front doors of Two Hearts Publishing.

The receptionist took one look at him . . . her . . . it . . . and gulped. "Can I . . . help . . . you?"

"Is there a mousy little woman named Lydia working here?"

"Yes. If you'll wait here, I'll—"

But Michael wasn't into waiting. "This is a personalized message. I have to give it in person." He pushed past the reception desk into the office area.

"Hey, you can't go back there! You're really not authorized—"

But it was too late. Michael was already out of earshot, scampering down the rows of cubicles where employees of the publishing company were toiling away.

He passed a cubicle bearing a little brass nameplate reading "Lydia Sinclair." The person inside had her back to him, but when she turned around, he could see that she was drab and pinched looking, with the least chic outfit and the worst haircut he'd ever seen on a woman outside of a prison or a mental hospital.

"You *must* be she!" he exclaimed. Lydia uttered a little bark of surprise when she saw the face, and the drag, and the balloons.

There was a platform piled with books outside Lydia Sinclair's office, and Michael scrambled up on top of it. Then, taking a pose, he began to belt out a medley from *Gypsy,* only with a change of lyrics. For a little man, he had an enormous voice, worthy of the Ethel Merman he aspired to be.

"Lydia, you've won the grand prize. Just think of it, all the movies you'll be watching free now . . . dramas, westerns, comedies, wow! Video Spot has the best selection . . . if you like porno, we're your connection . . . for you, Lydia! For free!"

Michael finished with a flourish, on a loud, long, high note, and jumped off the platform. "Our card," he announced grandly, handing her the whole handful of balloons with Video Spot's address and telephone number. And before the astonished girl could say a word, he was floating out on his high, narrow heels, down the corridor, through the reception area, and into the elevator.

Well, hell, if that didn't bring her in, nothing would. It had certainly been one of his better gigs. Michael personally knew people who would gladly pay $15.60 or more for a performance like that.

As it turned out, Michael's part was a lot easier than Jack's. Jack not only had to locate Parry, he had to convince him to come with him to the Video Spot. Parry could not conceive of leaving Lydia's office building without seeing her go out to lunch, and it took five minutes of red-faced arguing on Jack's part to get across the idea that Lydia would almost certainly not be going to a restaurant today. That there was every chance in the world that Parry would encounter her at the Video Spot.

But Parry was a creature of habit, and his habit was to be at the Haggensen Building every day at noon.

At first Jack argued with him, but in vain. At the end, though, the thing that finally wore down Parry's resistance was the magnificence of this new possession of his—he had Lydia's name. Lydia. Lydia Sinclair. Splendor. Music. Magic. Beauty. Euphony. Armed with this new talisman and the hope of seeing his lady up close, plus the promise of a hot home-cooked meal, Parry was at last content to trot across town to Eighth Avenue with Jack.

To Anne Napolitano, who had grown up in a house where soap was prized above everything except pasta and the Sacred Heart, the sight and the smell of

Parry came as a repulsive shock. You want to make a career as a bum, okay, but why not at least a *clean* bum? This wasn't going to work; what girl would look at a walking trash pile like him? But she kept her mouth shut, not wanting to rain on Jack's parade. She hadn't seen Jack this excited since . . . well, come to think of it, she'd *never* seen Jack this excited.

It was a quarter after twelve. Since Lydia operated like clockwork, if she was coming at all, she was due here in about five minutes. Jack would barely have time to slick back Parry's hair and pull a Video Spot T-shirt over Parry's head.

"See, with the shirt, it'll be like you work here," Jack assured him.

"What am I qualified to do?" Parry asked apprehensively. He was so nervous that his legs were trembling.

"Well, uh, just . . . stack up the tapes . . . sort 'em out . . . you know, in categories."

Parry's smell, though, was still the same. Very, very ripe. Like garbage left out for three days in the hot sun. In desperation, Jack looked around the store and came up with one of those pine-scented air fresheners that people hang in their cars, or in this case, on their cash registers. He held it in his hands, unsure what to do with it, and finally wound up hanging it around Parry's neck.

"This'll be good. This will make you smell like a pine forest."

At that moment the bell over the front door jingled and Lydia Sinclair walked in. Jack heard a gasp and a moan behind him and turned to see Parry swaying on his feet, his eyes closed. He was almost passing out.

"Parry, damn it! Keep it together!"

The small man nodded and forced his eyes open,

fixing them on Lydia as she came up to the counter. He'd never seen anything so wondrous as her beauty.

"Hello, my name is Lydia Sinclair," she said flatly, and Parry trembled all over with joy. He'd listened to her voice for the first time, and to him it was like the sonorous tolling of the bells of the cathedral of Notre Dame, or like the portentous harmonies of a Bach mass.

"Oh, hi, how ya doin'?" Jack was all smiles and affability. "Congratulations. I'm Jack Lucas. Nice to meet you finally. This is Anne Napolitano, owner of Video Spot."

"Hello," said Anne reluctantly. "Congratulations." She eyed Lydia curiously. This was the great beauty that Jack's little nutty pal was so crazy about? Yeah, well, crazy was the operative word here.

"And this," said Jack, drawing Parry forward by force, "is our . . . coworker . . . Parry . . . uh . . . Parry."

"Parry Parry?" Lydia asked, the most literal-minded person in the world. What a perfect companion for a man who saw Grails in magazine articles! They couldn't miss.

"No, just Parry," said Parry in a voice barely above a whisper.

"Oh, like Moses," Lydia said, and Parry gave a little hysterical moan, compounded of adoration and terror.

"So, how do we do this?" demanded the girl.

Jack thought a second. "Well, first you sign an official membership card." He took one from the pile by the register. "Just sign that, and we'll have this laminated for you right here. Parry. Would you like to laminate Miss Sinclair's card? Parry?"

It took him a minute to snap Parry out of his worshipful catatonia, but when the little man understood what was being asked of him, he took the card eagerly. For Lydia Sinclair, he'd laminate his tongue.

Just being in the same store with her, able to hear her speak, see her face up close, had sent him into such euphoria that he could barely function; the laminating machine was completely beyond his powers.

While Parry was reducing the membership card to a laminated tatter Anne was explaining the rules. "This will last you one year, after which you have the option to renew, if you like, at a membership discount."

"But now it's for free, right?" Lydia demanded suspiciously.

"Yeah," Anne admitted grudgingly. "Now it's for free."

"You can pick out up to ten movies—" Jack began.

"Free?" The girl might look like a mouse, but she was a mouth with sharp little teeth and a mighty suspicious mind.

"Yes, they're free."

"Only the first ten," Anne put in hastily. "After that, they're two-ninety-nine a rental."

Lydia turned this information over in her mind, looking for the catch. Then she headed for the shelves to check out the merchandise. Parry handed Jack the pathetic remnants of the laminated card, and Jack shook his head. Then all three turned to watch Lydia—Anne and Jack with curiosity and some amusement, Parry with his heart in his hopeful eyes.

Lydia pulled a videotape off the rack to have a look at it. Two others began to fall. She tried to catch them, and an entire rackful of videotapes began tumbling to the ground. Anne rolled her eyes in exasperation, and Jack nudged Parry forward to help. It took all the nerve Parry could muster to actually approach and speak to his beloved.

"Can . . . can I help you?"

Lydia turned. This odd little man was standing

very close to her, smelling of pine freshener. Proximity to another human being always made Lydia Sinclair uncomfortable. "No, no, I can look myself."

With your eyes closed, you could tell exactly where Lydia was in the store, by the crash of falling cassette boxes. Parry moved timidly behind her, like the sweeper after the circus parade, picking up the debris and stacking them back up. He held out a videotape.

"Hell Merchants?" he offered hopefully. "Good choice."

"I don't like horror movies," said Lydia flatly.

Nodding, Parry rummaged around for another. "How about this one?" He read from the blurb on the box. 'Zbigniew Speizak's *The Purple Bread,* an intensely portrayed tale of love and envy set against the sweeping background of a polish . . . uh . . . Polish . . . bakery. With subtitles."

Lydia Sinclair shook her head decisively. "I don't like Polish love stories. I like musicals."

Musicals! A preference at last! Parry's face brightened. "Well, we have plenty of those. Here's our entertainment center," and he gestured to a large filled rack. "We got Astaire and Rogers, Judy Garland, Al Jolson . . ."

"Got any Ethel Merman?"

"Ethel Merman . . . let's see." Parry pawed through the racks eagerly, then frantically. He came up empty. "Uh . . . we seem to be all out of Ethel Merman."

Lydia's face screwed up and a frustrated little scream came out of her. "What a gyp!" she shouted.

Jack nudged Anne in the side, a nudge that said plainly, Do something.

"You know," Anne lied, "I think I may have ordered some just the other day."

Think? May have? They didn't know whom they

were dealing with here. "Well, did you or didn't you?" demanded Lydia Sinclair.

Anne's eyes narrowed. "Yessss," she hissed. "They'll be in soon."

"Well, I guess I'll come back then," Lydia retorted prissily. She turned to leave.

"Miss Sinclair!" Jack called hastily. "Here's your card. Don't forget it." Anne handed her the laminated membership card. Lydia reached out to take it, and then she noticed Anne's fingernails. They were long, and red, and perfectly manicured. Each nail had a colorful painted star right in the middle of it. They were actually very beautiful, and Anne was quite proud of them.

"I like your nails," said Lydia, and her face softened just a little. "Where did you get them done?"

"Actually," Anne said with no small pride, "I do them myself. I used to work in a beauty parlor."

"I like the stars." Lydia's face was actually a little wistful, and suddenly she looked much younger.

A light bulb switched on over Jack Lucas's head. "You know, Anne does other people's nails, too." This was news to Anne, who gave him a surprised look, but before she could open her mouth, Jack said, "It's sort of a sideline. If you want, she could do *your* nails."

I'll kill him, thought Anne. The minute I get him alone, I'll tear him into tortellini. Then Lydia asked abruptly "How much?"

"Well," Jack began with a big smile, "since you're a member, we could—"

"Forty dollars," Anne interrupted firmly.

"Forty dollars?" Jack squeaked.

Lydia Sinclair scrunched her face up as though she were in physical pain. Her nose twitched like a squirrel, and she muttered under her breath, "Forty . . . uh . . . fort—" The thought of parting with so much money was evidently giving her a severe ache in the gut. She mentally calculated the impact that forty dollars would make on her budget. Parry watched her, not daring to breathe or even blink his eyes.

"Okay, forty dollars," she said at last. Jack's eyebrows went up in surprise, and Parry let his breath out in a whistle. "When will you do them?"

Anne considered. She was already regretting the turn events were taking. She really didn't want to get sucked into this any more than she was already. "I don't know. Maybe next—"

"Tonight?" Parry suggested.

"Tonight?" echoed Jack, and on his face was a look of pleading mingled with hope. Anne shot him a dirty look.

"Tonight," said Lydia Sinclair in her flat voice.

"Tonight," agreed Anne, with a sigh.

Fourteen

"You know, getting your nails done is one thing, but going to dinner with a bunch of strangers and—" Anne broke off and threw a significant glance at Parry. "*This* one, well, Lydia's not gonna buy it. She didn't even look at him."

Parry didn't appear to be listening to Anne's scathing commentary. He held out his plate for more macaroni and smiled winningly. "Thank you."

But Anne Napolitano wasn't won over. She was far from happy about having this certified lunatic sitting at her table eating her out of house and home, and much less than enthused by Jack's crazy plan of getting the four of them together tonight for dinner.

"It won't be like a real date," Jack said over his shoulder. His voice was muffled because his head was in the closet, where he was rummaging for something decent for Parry to wear. "We're going to make it real casual."

"Got any more starchy food?" Parry asked brightly. With a little scowl, Anne got up from the table and went into the kitchen for the casserole dish. Parry's eyes followed her, appreciating the bouncing of her large breasts and the rotating motion of her hips underneath the tight skirt. All woman, his eyes said.

"I mean, I've gone out with bums," Anne added, dumping the remainder of the macaroni from the dish into Parry's plate, "but they were beautiful. It's the only reason to go out with a bum."

"This food's delicious." Parry beamed. "You're a wonderful cook. and you have a lovely set of . . . dishes."

Anne looked startled and repulsed. "Jack, he's trying to start a conversation with me!" she bawled.

"Well, talk back. He won't bite you."

She drew in a deep breath, which made her prominent breasts stand out even more. "Thank you," she said as politely as she could.

"You're welcome," Parry replied with equal ceremony, happily wolfing down the chow. He kept his admiring eyes on Anne. "You know, you're a beautiful woman. You got your own business. I'm surprised some guy doesn't snatch you up all for his own."

Anne sneaked a look over at Jack, but he was still busy sorting through his wardrobe. *"You're* surprised! But I guess I just never met the right guy. Whaddya gonna do?"

Parry put down his spoon. "I'm shocked! With a childbearing body like yours, why, a guy would have to be out of his mind!"

"Most guys are," Anne observed dryly.

Parry warmed up to his topic. "This is outrageous!" he declared. "No! You, this incredible woman, going to waste before my eyes! I will not hear of this!" Rising to his feet, he swept the food, the dishes, and everything off the table with one broad movement of his arm. Anne uttered a little squeak of disbelief and fear.

"Come on! I'm your man! Let's do it right here! Let's go to that place of splendor in the grass!"

"Jack!" Anne yelled in horror. Nothing this insane had ever happened to her before. She began to back away from the table, looking around her wildly for help.

Parry climbed up on the table and unzipped his pants. "Behold!" he cried proudly, about to grab hold of his little guy. "My magic wand! Come, free your golden orbs!"

"Jack!"

"Holdin' my penis," crooned Parry, serenading this beautiful woman. "What a wonderful way of sayin' how much you like me—"

"What are you, out of your mind? Jack!"

"Parry! Close your pants," Jack ordered quietly, coming in holding a suit on a hanger.

"Took you long enough." Parry grinned, zipping up his trousers. He turned to Anne. "But you let me know. You're too good a woman to go to waste."

Anne drew in a ragged breath. Could you believe this guy? One minute nuts, the next minute . . . almost making sense.

Jack paid no attention to any of this. By now he was used to Parry and his wild mood swings. He held the suit up in front of Parry and cast a critical eye over it. "What are you, a size forty in a jacket?"

Gathering up the suit, a shirt, and a tie, Jack led Parry downstairs. The Video Spot was closed for the evening, and the back room would be the perfect place to get Parry ready for his not-like-a-real-date with Lydia Sinclair. And Parry would no doubt take a lot of getting ready.

Anne cleared the crockery up from the floor and carried the broken dishes and the cutlery into the kitchen. She washed them and scoured the casserole and wiped down the table, the sink, and the stove, but her mind wasn't on her chores. She was thinking about Jack, about the amazing effect that this nut Parry seemed to be having on him.

Partly, Anne felt hurt—why did her lover prefer spending his time with a schizophrenic street bum rather than with her? She knew that he felt guilty about what had happened to Parry's life, but somehow she got the idea that Jack actually almost enjoyed looking after Parry, that something other than guilt was operating here.

But, also, Anne was fascinated, both drawn to and repelled by this crazy little man. Underneath all that horse shit there had to be a pony. Parry was obviously intelligent, and not all that bad to look at, if you scraped off the thick layers of crud he was hiding under. He had beautiful eyes and a warm, sweet smile. And there was a kind of interaction between him and Jack that intrigued her; this was a side of Jack Lucas that Anne had never seen, a kind of emerging gentleness, as though Parry were a child that needed looking after. And what about Lydia? *There* was a character! A mouse on the outside, a tiger on the inside. And covered with prickly thorns like a little hedgehog. Lydia Sinclair was somebody who couldn't face life unless her back was to the wall, but once she did, watch out, life! Parry found this homely girl with knobby knees and protruding elbows gorgeous. He gazed at her drab face and nothing hair and stick figure and saw a movie star. She hung the moon for him, and Anne, who was under her tough exterior a mushy romantic, found that ineffably touching. Lydia didn't know how lucky she was; if only Jack would look at *her* that way. Naaah, she was dreaming. Never happen.

When she'd finished in the kitchen, Anne laid out all her manicure implements and nail paints on a clean cloth on the coffee table. She was brushing her hair when the doorbell rang, and she opened the door to find Lydia Sinclair standing outside with a suspicious, rather fearful expression on her face.

"Hello, welcome." Anne greeted her with as much warmth as she could muster. "Come in."

But Lydia lingered half in and half out of the doorway, as if afraid of what she might find inside. Anne put one hand on her hip impatiently, and Lydia crossed the threshold at last. She looked around the apartment with undisguised curiosity.

"I've never been inside an apartment over a store before," she said in that flat monotone of hers. "You always walk past them when you walk by, but you never think anybody really lives in them."

Stung, Anne opened her mouth to say something sarcastic, then thought better of it. After all, it wasn't as though Lydia was going to make any difference in her life. After tonight, Anne would never see this prickly person again. She could afford to be nice.

"Can I get you anything? A little coffee, a little tea, maybe? Or how about a little tequila?"

"No, thank you." Lydia was eyeing the tools spread out on the table. She saw nail files, clippers, little manicure scissors, all of them gleaming cold steel like surgical instruments. They looked efficient and almost deadly.

"Will it . . . hurt?" she asked timidly.

"That all depends on you. Sure you don't want a drink?"

"Uh . . . maybe."

Fetching the bottle of tequila, Anne poured them both a healthy shot, and she led Lydia to the sofa.

"You'll enjoy this," Jack assured Parry, slathering an Ernest Lazlo mudpack all over Parry's anxious little face. "This is great for you. It'll make you feel good."

Parry fidgeted nervously, his eyes squinched tight shut. "Mud? You just washed that off."

"That was a different kind of mud. This will make you look great."

"Oh, it's good mud." Parry struggled to understand.

"Just leave it on for a while. It's gonna make a big difference, you'll see," Jack told him. "Now, some clothes. How about this?'' He held up a Gianni Versace linen suit, white with black stripes, that had set him back close to two grand in his earlier life. It was way too big for Parry, especially in the length of the trousers, but Jack thought he could make it work. A staple gun and a few dozen staples ought to do the trick. ''Just relax,'' he instructed Parry, although he could see that it was an impossible task. The man was so antsy, he couldn't stop jittering.

''Will you hold still so I can do this?'' Jack demanded, trying not to staple Parry's flesh to the linen.

''I'm sorry. I'm just so excited! You must have felt this way when you first met Anne, huh?''

Jack didn't reply. He wished that Parry wouldn't keep harping on his relationship with Anne Napolitano. It stirred up guilt feelings in Jack he didn't enjoy.

''Yeah, if I wasn't already committed to Lydia, boy . . .'' said Parry enthusiastically. ''Except Anne would never go for me, though. She loves you too much. And you really love her, huh?''

Jack didn't know how to answer this.

''You love her a lot, Jack,'' Parry reassured him. ''You're crazy about her. It's just that . . . sometimes . . . you're a little bit of an asshole.''

Jack looked up, startled, from his stapling. Now why did he have the feeling that Parry had hit the nail on the head?

''So?'' asked Anne, pushing Lydia's cuticles back with an orange stick. ''Anybody special in your life?''

Lydia pulled her hand out of Anne's and took the other hand out of the liquid in which it was soaking. ''Does it look like there's anybody special in my life?'' she retorted defensively. She took another sip of her tequila.

"Don't say it like that," Anne said, grabbing the hand back. "It's not such a crazy idea. You're a healthy woman. You hold a steady job. You're not cross-eyed or anything—"

"Well, there's nobody special," Lydia snapped, but her eyes clouded.

"Okay, fine." Anne shrugged. It was no skin off her ass. She was just trying to make conversation.

Lydia nibbled on her lower lip. "I mean, it's not easy in this day and age."

"What's not easy?" Anne picked up the emery board and smoothed the edges of Lydia's nails.

"Meeting people."

Anne grinned. "Oh, Gawd, tell me about it. I've been dating longer than I've been driving." As the truth of her own remark struck her she laughed. "I can't believe that."

Lydia's voice dropped to a whisper. "I have never really . . . been through a . . . dating period . . ." she confessed.

"It's a disgusting process," Anne assured her. "You haven't missed anything."

Lydia nodded a little dubiously, and Anne could tell that she didn't really believe her, that she thought she'd missed out on a great deal. Both of them raised their glasses again, draining them. Anne refilled them.

The manicure wasn't going so badly after all. Once Lydia was convinced that Anne wasn't going to murder her, and once the tequila began to take hold, Lydia loosened up a bit and began to confide in Anne. They were just girls together, after all, and this was just girl talk, nothing more.

"My mother calls me once a week," Lydia said, hitting the tequila glass again. "Like a recurring nightmare. 'So, have you met anyone?' 'No,

Mother.' 'So, what's going to happen?' 'I don't know, Mother.' I only thank God I moved out.''

"I can't believe you lived with your mother for so many years," said Anne. "If I had to live with *my* mother, I'd stab myself six times.''

Lydia sighed and looked thoughtful, rolling her glass in one hand, while Anne worked on the other, and staring down into the depths of the golden liquor. "I think some people are meant to be alone," she said finally. "This is my idea. I was born a man in a former life and I used women for pleasure, and now I'm paying for it." She sighed again. "I wouldn't mind so much if I could just remember the pleasure parts.''

Anne finished painting Lydia's right hand and reached for the left. "Mind the nails; they're wet. I think you're getting a little complicated. What in your opinion is the actual problem?''

Lydia thought the question over gravely. "I don't feel like I make any impression on people," she said slowly, slurring her words. "I don't think I have any personality. At office parties all I do is rearrange the hors d'oeuvres while people are eating them so the platters look as though they're still full. I don't start conversations, because . . . I don't know how to make them end or where to make them go.''

Shaking her head, Anne advised, "You gotta be a little easier on yourself, doll. A conversation has a life of its own. I mean, look at us. We're having a conversation.''

"I'm paying you," Lydia said bluntly.

Hurt and angry, Anne let Lydia's hand fall. "Will you stop it! I'm not like that. I don't do people favors. If I talk to you, it's because I want to. All right, you're not a super-model," she continued, putting it mildly. "We can't all be Jerry Hall. What a boring world it would be if we were all Jerry Hall. So you do the best with what you got.'' She thought a minute; her brain was a little fuzzy from the drink. "You want to make an impression? You're looking for a personality? Try this on for size. You can be a real bitch!"

Lydia gasped and her eyes snapped open. She struggled with the concept for a moment, and then her face lit up. "A bitch! Me? Really?"

"You bet."

"Wow!"

As he saw the preparations coming to an end Parry became more and more agitated. He couldn't stand still. He kept fidgeting while Jack tried to calm him down, tying his tie again to get a better knot, smoothing the rather crumpled lapels of the linen suit that had been crushed in the closet.

Jack stepped back to get a better look at Parry. Well, *GQ* would never put him on the cover, but he looked a lot better than the old Parry in rags. For one thing, he was clean, as clean as Jack could get him, considering that some of the grime had been there so long it had worked its way under Parry's skin. His face was gleaming from the mudpack, and his unruly wiry hair had been brushed down with a little bit of mousse. The suit still fit him funny; it was way, way too big, but look who his date would be! They'd be two small people hiding in their clothing. All in all, Jack Lucas was pretty proud of his handiwork.

"I'm gonna give you my wallet so you can pay for dinner," he said, tucking it into Parry's breast pocket.

"You're a nice man, Jack, doing all this for me."

Jack only grunted, his eye going over the last details to see if he could make them better. Suddenly he felt Parry's arms wrapped tightly around him, and Parry's terrified voice whispering in his ear, "I'm scared, Jack."

Extricating himself from the embrace, Jack took a good look at Parry. He *did* look scared; in fact, he looked so scared he was almost ill with it.

"I feel so much for her . . . I feel like something awful is going to happen."

"Nothing awful's gonna happen," said Jack reassuringly, patting Parry's shoulder awkwardly. He wasn't much good at this comforting stuff. "Anne'll be there. I'll be there. Nothing awful's gonna happen."

"I'm still scared," Parry whispered.

Jack took a long look at him, and a stab of pity cut through him like a knife. "I know," he whispered back. It's gonna be fine. You're lookin' good."

"Okay." Parry nodded, making an effort to get a grip.

"Just remember to breathe," said Jack.

"I gotta breathe."

"*Big* breaths."

Fifteen

Jack and Parry could hear the sound of women's hysterical laughter all the way up the stairs. It caught Parry off balance, and he lagged behind Jack, uncertain.

Jack pushed the apartment door open and his mouth dropped open in astonishment. Lydia Sinclair was rolling around on the floor. Literally on her back on the floor, her hands held high in the air to keep her nails dry, and she was hooting with laughter. There was color in her cheeks. Tears of mirth put a sparkle in her eye and her drab hair was attractively mussed. Perched on a hassock next to the coffee table was Anne Napolitano, red in the face from laughing so hard. Jack took one look at the half-empty tequila bottle and the two empty glasses, and his face broke into a knowing grin. The girls had been having themselves a party.

"Hi, how's it going?"

At the sound of Jack's voice Lydia started guiltily. She sat up at once and an immediate change came over her. She stopped laughing, becoming the old Lydia Sinclair again, as she retreated into her customary shy, self-protective shell. Her face closed tightly, and her expression was pinched and a little frightened.

"Parry," said Jack, a bit too loudly, "It's Lydia Sinclair, our membership winner."

"I know!" Parry glowed. He was still afraid to

actually come into the apartment, but Jack gave him a tug.

"What are you two up to?" asked Anne, on cue.

"Well," Jack drawled too casually, "everything's locked up downstairs. We thought we'd get some dinner." He raised his voice, as though he'd just hit upon a brilliant idea. "Say! Anybody up for Chinese?" He'd chosen Chinese food specifically to tempt Lydia, because she already liked it. Looking straight at her, he "had" another brilliant idea. "Have you eaten? Would you like to join us?"

Acutely uncomfortable now, Lydia got to her feet. "Oh, no, I'd rather go home." It was the perfect Lydia Sinclair tactless response.

"Me too," Parry said fervently, and Jack dug his elbow sharply into the small man's ribs. This was not the time to chicken out.

"The nails!" Anne yelled, alarmed. "Watch the nails! Listen," she added persuasively, "you still have to eat."

"No, really, I gotta go home." Lydia's face was screwed up into that old sour knot again.

"Hey, what did I tell you?" Anne spoke to her like a big sister; the kid wasn't so bad after all, not when you got to know her. "Why don't you come? It's just dinner." She grinned at the girl. "You'll have something to tell your mother next time she calls."

A small smile attempted to escape Lydia's tightly pressed lips, but it failed. She still shook her head no.

Time to show a little Italian muscle, make the offer that can't be refused. *"You . . . are . . . coming!"* Anne thundered. And it was settled.

It was another lovely evening; the moon played peekaboo with the clouds, and even New York's seamy underbelly didn't look too bad when bathed in moonlight. The four of them cut over toward the river, walking in pairs. Parry and Lydia went on ahead, Jack strolling a few steps behind with Anne, to give the other two a chance to get acquainted.

Jack kept a sharp eye on the couple in front. Lydia hadn't seemed to notice that Parry's suit was way too big for him, or that his sleeves and trouser legs were pinned up with staples, or that his train of thought occasionally jumped the track. Who knows? This date just might work out, after all. As Anne said, stranger things have been known to happen. When Anne rubbed her shoulder against him and slipped her hand into his, Jack gave her fingers a grateful little squeeze.

"What do you do?" Parry asked. It was more than polite conversation. Every scrap of information about Lydia was a tiny little treasure to be stored up, and laid out later on the altar of his heart and on the altar in his room.

"I work in a publishing house," Lydia replied. "Two Hearts Publishing. I . . . uh . . . I get to read some of the books, but mostly I calculate the production costs from first-edition hardcover into softcover. After that, it's basically someone else's problem."

"It sounds exciting," said Parry in an admiring voice. He was transported, in silent raptures, almost unable to contain his joy. To be walking beside the most wonderful, beautiful, intelligent girl in all the world! How did he deserve this? He could almost not stand so much happiness!

"Why does it sound exciting?" Lydia demanded. "There's absolutely nothing exciting about it at all."

Spotting something on the street, Parry bent to pick it up. He thrust the bit of refuse behind his back and kept his hands behind him, busily working.

His answer was heartfelt and earnestly expressed. "Well, you're calculating costs that could have an effect on whether or not a book is published. And if it is published, it could be a book that might somehow change the way that people think or act. A book can do that.''

''We mostly publish trashy romance novels,'' Lydia said matter-of-factly.

''Don't ever say that!'' Parry turned to her, glowing with emotion. ''There's nothing trashy about romance. In romance there's passion . . . it's beauty and magic . . . and besides, you can find some wonderful things in the trash.''

Bringing his hands around from behind his back, he held out his palm for Lydia to see. In it was a charming little piece of furniture, no more than two inches high. Parry had found a champagne cork, the real kind—not plastic—but the kind with the thin metal wire wrapped around it. By twisting the wire, Parry had created a tiny chair, a miniature treasure. Smiling, he offered it to Lydia.

She accepted Parry's gift with pleasure, returning his smile, and there was a look of wonderment on her face. In the moonlight, contemplating her little chair, she could almost be taken for beautiful.

The Chinese restaurant was quite large, and much fancier than the one near Lydia's office. This room had red flocked walls and gold wooden trim on the banquettes, and little colored lanterns with gold-and-red tassels hanging from the ceiling. The four of them took a large corner booth and decided that Jack would give the order.

They sat pretty much in silence until the food came; Lydia and Parry were too shy and uncomfortable to speak, and their feelings of anxiety communicated themselves to Jack and Anne. So far, though, everything seemed to be going okay. Parry had not tried to unzip his pants, and Lydia had not run shrieking out into the night. The waiter arrived at last, placed plates and chopsticks in front of everybody, and a tray of covered dishes was transferred to the table.

Anne took the cover off the first dish. "Oh, dumplings!" she exclaimed. "I could eat all of these."

"Would you like a dumpling?" Jack asked Lydia politely.

"Yes, please."

"There we go." He spooned several onto Lydia's plate.

Nervously, the girl picked up her chopsticks. Her experience with dumplings and Chinese chopsticks had so far been all bad. She loved them, but they always eluded her. They were hard enough to handle even when her nails hadn't been freshly varnished. But with the new manicure, dumplings were a catastrophe waiting to happen, and Lydia didn't find it reassuring that this guy Parry didn't take his eyes off her. His staring, and the company of strangers, made her even more self-conscious, and inevitably the first slippery dumpling wound up not in her plate but in her lap.

"Oh, God," she muttered, mortified.

Instantly, Parry picked up *his* dumpling and dropped it deliberately into *his* lap. "Oh, boy. Sorry."

Her face scarlet, Lydia dipped her napkin into her glass and began to scrub at her skirt. Parry scrubbed at his trousers with his wet napkin. When Lydia knocked her water glass over, flooding the table, Parry knocked his water glass over, flooding the floor.

"Oh, I'm so clumsy, please forgive me," he said to Lydia. "I do everything wrong. You're so patient."

Lydia looked startled, then she relaxed a little, relieved that somebody at the table was clumsier than she was and that she wasn't the center of attention.

Jack marveled at the girl's density; Parry's little ploy was so transparent, yet Lydia didn't catch on. She was so nervous and self-preoccupied that she didn't notice that his every clumsy movement was a mirror image of her own.

The meal progressed. Other courses were served, and other problems were encountered by Lydia and countered by Parry. When Lydia put her face in her food and didn't bother to look up or make conversation, Parry mimicked her exactly. When Lydia had trouble separating the lo mein noodles and sat there with them hanging out of her mouth, Parry did the same. There was the most enormous smile all over his face, from his hair to his bearded chin. He was living out his fantasy, the knight coming to the rescue of the damsel in distress.

To Jack, Parry appeared to be having the time of his life. He felt a warm little glow of satisfaction; this was all his idea, and he'd made it happen. He'd done pretty good, he told himself. For once in his life he seemed to have done the right thing.

"What do you think?" he asked Anne in an undertone.

Anne grinned. "I think they're made for each other," she whispered back. "And I think it's scary," she added.

By the time the dishes were almost empty, a feeling of mellowness had settled over the table. Anne had cracked a few of her jokes, and Lydia had actually laughed. Her unexpectedly raucous laughter had a contagious effect on all of them, and soon the four of them were giggling and chuckling at almost every dumb thing that was said. They laughed over the little mottoes in the fortune cookies; they laughed when Parry took out Jack's wallet and fumbled through the bills to get the right amount for the check. They even laughed when Anne picked up half of the outrageous tip that Parry had left and stuffed it back into the wallet. It was one of those uncommon golden moments in life when everything is funny and there are friends around to share the joke.

Now they sat for a minute, replete, satisfied, knowing that they had to get up and leave the restaurant, but somehow reluctant to break this moment off. Then Parry began to sing, in a sweet, low voice. It was a comic song, an old music-hall and vaudeville ditty made popular by the great Groucho Marx, a song about a tattooed lady named Lydia. He sang it directly to Lydia and there was no mistaking his meaning. Even though the lyrics were absurd, it was a love song of the greatest tenderness.

Then the song came to an end. Silence fell over them, but it wasn't unpleasant, only peaceful.

At last, Parry broke the silence. "I'd like to take you home tonight. Would it be all right?" he asked tentatively. Lydia turned her face away, but she nodded.

Jack and Anne walked home very slowly, enjoying the evening. They were in a remarkably good mood, the first time their moods had actually coincided in many weeks. Recalling the meal, and Parry's hilarious attempts to keep up with Lydia's blunderings, they laughed so hard that they had to hold on to each other to keep from falling over.

"When . . . the noodles were hanging out of her mouth . . . I thought I was gonna die. . . ." Anne giggled, wiping tears of hilarity from her eyes.

"How about when Parry was digging in his lap for the piece of broccoli—" Jack gasped.

"Oh, God, yes, the broccoli—" and they exploded in fresh shrieks of laughter. "And, when the lichee nut rolled off the table—"

"No more, I can't take any more," Jack pleaded. "My sides hurt like hell."

They subsided and strolled along together quietly.

Then Anne said, in a wistful voice. "I'm actually very surprised. She seemed to go for him. Guess there's somebody for everybody, huh?"

"You know? I can't believe I did it," Jack mused. He was very tired, but it was worth all the effort and strain he'd put into this stunt. He felt good about himself.

It seemed to him now that he'd made Parry happy. And if Parry was happy, if Parry got what he wanted, then Jack would be off the hook. Free and clear. No more guilt, no more listening to Parry's ravings about the Holy Grail. Jack could get on with his life, Parry with his. Also, the little guy deserved some happiness, and Jack was suddenly glad that he was the one to help give it to him.

But there was something more. Seeing the intensity and the purity of Parry's unconditional love for Lydia had an odd effect on Jack. It made him envious. Who'd think that someone like Jack Lucas would envy a schizo street bum? What irony. Although, since Parry had entered Jack's life, it had become a walking irony.

"Amor vincit omnia," Anne said suddenly. "It's Latin," she explained when Jack shot a questioning look at her. "It means 'love conquers all.' I don't mean us," she added hastily. "I mean everybody else. Not us."

"Do you think it will work out?" Jack asked softly. They had reached the store, and Anne pulled the key to the door to their upstairs apartment from her purse.

Her face grew thoughtful. "Who knows? Two people can be in the same room at a party and never see each other. Two other people can be on opposite sides of the world, and nothing can keep them apart. If a thing is meant to happen, it'll—what?" She broke off as she caught Jack smiling at her.

"You were great tonight," he said softly. "Thanks

a lot." There was more affection in his tone than
Anne had heard in a good long while, and it thrilled
her. She unlocked the door, feeling warm inside,
then she turned to him, and her large black eyes
looked seriously into his.

"You did a great thing for somebody tonight,"
she told him sincerely. "I was really proud to be
with you."

Jack reached for Anne's hand and brought it up to
his lips. The gesture surprised him as much as it did
her; it was so uncharacteristic of him to be romantic.
Then he pulled her into his arms, first kissing her
tenderly, and then with rising passion. Joyfully, Anne
threw her arms tightly around him and returned his
kiss. Their ardor increased with the pressure of their
bodies, and mingled until it grew too overwhelming
for them to withstand. Moaning with pleasure, unwilling to break off their caresses, they barely made
it up the stairs and into the bedroom, where they fell
on each other with hunger.

"Tell me about yourself," Parry begged. "I want
to know everything."

Lydia shrugged. "There's nothing to tell."

"Don't say that." They had almost reached her
apartment building.

Lydia turned to look at Parry, one of the few times
she'd allowed him to see her face. "No, really, this
is it."

"Well, it's enough for me," Parry stated loyally.

"You don't have to say that." Lydia cast her eyes
down and turned her face away again.

"I never say anything I have to."

The girl fumbled awkwardly with the strap of her
purse, tying it into little knots as she spoke. "I
mean, you don't have to say nice things to me. It's
a little old-fashioned considering what we're about
to do."

"What are we about to do?" Parry asked, genuinely puzzled.

This was very hard for Lydia, and she stammered a little. "Well, you're taking me home. I . . . think . . . you're sort of . . . attracted to me—"

"Yes!" breathed Parry.

"You'll probably want to come upstairs . . . for coffee—"

"I don't drink coffee."

"—and then we'll probably have a drink . . . and talk . . . and get to know each other a little better . . . and get comfortable . . . and we'll . . . we'll . . . then you'll sleep over . . . and then . . . in the morning . . . you'll awake, and you'll be distant . . . and you won't be able . . . to stay for coffee—"

"I don't drink coffee," said Parry again.

But Lydia wasn't listening. She was deep inside her own pain, dredging up the memories of one-nighters, past rejections. "And then we'll exchange phone numbers and you'll leave and never call." Her eyes were haunted by her anguish. "And I'll go to work and I'll feel so *good* for the first hour, and then, ever so slowly, I'll turn into a piece of dirt."

Parry gazed at her, his face tender and soft with sympathy.

"Why am I putting myself through this?" she asked suddenly, snapping out of the past. She turned, running up the stairs of her brownstone, then she turned back to Parry as she remembered her manners. "It was really nice to meet you. Good night." And she headed for the front door.

"Excuse me! Wait! Wait! Wait up! 'Scuse me! Wait!" Parry yelled after Lydia a little desperately.

She turned back reluctantly. "Listen, I'm not feeling well—" she began.

"Well, no wonder. We just met, made love, and broke off all in the space of thirty seconds, and I can't even remember the first kiss, which is the best part.'' Lydia was standing several steps above him, in the light coming from the downstairs hallway of her house. Parry looked up at her face, and it seemed to him even more radiant than ever.

Lydia had never intended to open herself up to this stranger. She wanted desperately to go home now. ''Listen, it really was very special to meet you—'' she began with some awkwardness.

''I think you should shut up now,'' Parry interrupted. ''Shut up, please. Thank you. I'm not coming up to your apartment,'' he told her earnestly. ''That was never my intention.''

The young woman's face reddened with humiliation. ''Oh, God, you mean you don't want to—''

''Oh, no, I want to,'' Parry assured her. ''I've got a hard-on for you the size of Florida . . . but . . . I don't want . . . just one night. I have a confession I have to make to you.''

''You're married?'' A spasm of anxiety crossed her face at the thought of it.

''No.''

''Divorced?''

''No.''

''You have a disease?''

''No, please stop!'' Parry came up two of the steps that separated him from Lydia and laid his hand gently over her mouth before she could speak again. He looked deeply into her eyes and in a voice so quiet she almost missed the words, Parry said, ''I'm in love with you.''

Lydia gasped.

''It's not just from tonight. I've known you for a long time,'' he continued softly. Lydia's eyes widened and she listened in astonishment. ''I know that you come out of work at noon every day. I see you fight your way out of that revolving door, and you're pushed back inside. And three seconds later you come out again. I walk with you to lunch. I know that on Wednesday you go to that dim sum parlor. I know what you order. And I know it's a good day if you stop and get that romance novel. I see you buying jawbreakers before you go back in to work.''

Slowly, he removed his hand from her mouth, but Lydia remained silent, just staring at Parry in fascination. Nothing like this had ever happened to her before; it was the epitome of every romance novel she'd ever devoured, it was the epitome of every romantic dream she'd secretly harbored. As she listened tears welled up in her eyes and rolled one by one down her cheeks.

''I know you hate your job, and you don't have many friends, and maybe you're a little . . . uncoordinated . . . but . . . alone as you are . . . I love you.'' The joy in Parry's breast was so strong he thought he'd burst with it. This was a moment he never expected to happen. He used to think he'd be following his lady around, half a block behind her, for the rest of his life! And now, here he was, telling the woman he loved what was in his heart, and she was actually listening! He smiled broadly. ''I love you! I think you're the greatest thing since spice racks and I would be knocked out several times just to have that first kiss. But, oh, I'll be back in the morning. And I won't be distant. And I will call if you let me. But I still don't drink coffee.''

The two of them stood looking at each other in a mist of wonder. Parry didn't see a homely, skinny girl, and Lydia didn't see a crazy man in a suit so large it had to be stapled. They looked into each other's eyes and they saw each other's hearts. And what each of them found made both of them happy.

Slowly, Lydia came down the brownstone steps toward Parry. She brought her face close to his and kissed him. It was an awkward, tentative kiss, nothing practiced or erotic about it, but to Parry it was the kiss of an angel. He trembled all over his small body. With infinitely gentle fingers, he brushed the tears out of his darling's eyes.

Then, Lydia being Lydia, she pinched his cheek skeptically, quite hard. He flinched.

"You are real . . . aren't you?" she whispered, lost in amazement.

Parry nodded, and they kissed again, like two innocent children, their lips touching as lightly as butterflies sip nectar from a flower.

She backed away from him slowly, then turned and ran lightly up the stairs of her house. At the top she turned and spoke, and Parry had never heard that abrasive voice utter sounds so sweet. "You can call me," she said.

Then, Lydia being Lydia, she tried to get into her house through the locked half of the door, and it took her a little more fumbling to make a semigraceful exit.

Parry didn't even notice the blunder. He stood there, dazzled. What an historical moment, a time of exaltation! Even if Lydia had forgotten to give him her telephone number, he knew where to find her. And she would be waiting. God, he was happy! He was so happy he could . . . no, wait! What was that sound? Something was watching him. He could feel it; he could almost taste it. Something hideous and terrifying was waiting for him in the darkness. Something knew he was alone; something knew he was unarmed; something was sensing Parry's vulnerability at this very moment and was lurking hungrily to feed on it.

And Parry knew what that something was. It was the Red Knight.

Sixteen

He was out there; Parry was aware of him with all his senses. He was out there, very close by, and he was totally aware of Parry, too. Parry stood, paralyzed with fear. Now he thought he could hear it, the pounding of the war-horse's iron hooves, and a neighing that grew so loud it split his eardrums. His very nostrils could smell the animal's breath. Very, very slowly, knowing what was waiting there, but afraid to look, Parry turned his head.

They'd come. They were on the corner, sitting horse and rider. The Red Knight's sword was drawn, was raised high in his mailed fist. Flames as red as blood streamed from his helmet and down along the iron of his armor, turning it incarnadine. He was the living fire incarnate, the Red Knight, and he knew that Parry was alone. For a long time he'd been waiting for Jack to go away; the Red Knight was afraid of Jack Lucas, but he wasn't afraid of Parry. He was Parry's deadliest enemy. Long ago, he'd sworn to rip out Parry's heart with the point of his lance and to split open Parry's skull with his sword.

Most of all, the Red Knight intended to take away by force anything that Parry needed to survive. They'd met a very long time ago, these two, in another life, and at that time the Red Knight had been triumphant. He'd taken it all, leaving only emptiness and deadly secrets.

Yet Parry had managed to survive, God only knew

how. He'd fled the secrets, going deep down into that emptiness to exist for a while, and out of that emptiness he'd fashioned a new life for himself. It wasn't a good life, or a happy life, but Parry had survived.

When he learned of Parry's survival, the Red Knight had been furiously angry; his war-horse had stamped his feet so loudly the earth had cracked and crumbled; great pits had opened, yawning, beneath those hooves. The raging flames that came issuing from the Red Knight's helmed face and armor had magnified and swelled until they extinguished the sun and exploded into the sky. He swore vengeance; he swore annihilation. Parry would never escape him again.

Since that time, the enemy was never far away; Parry was always conscious of his malevolent threatening presence somewhere at the periphery of his new life. The Red Knight was the very personification of evil and cruelty, those things that Parry tried so hard to combat, but every way he turned, the Red Knight blocked him with his horrific power. Many times he had seen him, and always—except once—Parry had been terribly afraid. Only that one time in Central Park when Jack was with him did the Red Knight give ground, turn, and run away. What a glorious moment that had been!

Over time Parry had learned and devised mysterious rituals for keeping the Red Knight at a distance—magic charms and incantations that usually worked. The most powerful incantation was *Don't think. Don't remember.* There were certain secret things Parry didn't dare to think about, secrets buried so deeply in the core of him that he successfully forgot them . . . most of the time. These were hidden things of such hazardous import that their revelation would destroy his world. The Red Knight was the designated keeper of those secrets; they formed the power of his sword and his lance, they were the fulcrum of his evil might.

Tonight, Parry had made a fatal mistake; he'd been happy. Being with Lydia had made him happy. He'd forgotten the first and most important rule. Never let them see you happy. He'd allowed the forbidden feeling not only to enter his heart, but to suffuse him entirely. He'd radiated with his joy, and the Red Knight had detected the glow and come riding hard to extinguish it. How could he have been so foolish as to have forgotten? It might cost him everything.

Knowing that Parry was weak and vulnerable tonight because he was happy and not on his guard, the Red Knight had come to strike the fatal blow. Parry had been a fool to think that he could hold on to this newfound happiness with Lydia, that the Red Knight had not been out there watching and waiting. Waiting for his chance, ready and armed to take this new joy away, too, and leave only the emptiness behind.

The most fearful thing of all was that Parry knew exactly how it would happen. He could already feel the lance point in his heart, already feel his skull sliced open by the flaming sword, to expose his insides and fill them with the Red Knight's terrible secrets, which Parry had once hurled far away from himself and which he didn't dare remember.

The horse reared, its hooves cracking through the sky, but the Red Knight reined him in and turned his head forward. His flaming spurs bit deeply into the war steed's back, below the chain mail. Horse and rider moved slowly at first, but Parry knew that was deceptive. Very soon now, they'd be galloping, charging directly at him, like the portrait in Parry's room. Flames would billow out of them, obscuring the outlines of knight and steed, so that it would appear as though a juggernaut of pure fire was racing to the kill.

Parry whimpered in fear. "Let me have this," he

pleaded in a whisper. "Please let me have this."
Even though he knew better than to ask.

The trot became a gallop; the Red Knight was
coming closer. *"Let me have this!"* Parry roared in
desperation. Tears came pouring out of his eyes and
down his cheeks, wetting his beard. He fell to his
knees, sobbing.

But he knew it was of no use; the Red Knight was
implacable, he'd sworn an oath to Parry's destruc-
tion. Parry was to have nothing, nothing ever again.
He was to die instead. He should run, but his legs
wouldn't move. His mouth opened to scream, but no
sound came out, and his lips formed the circle of a
terrified "no."

Now the Red Knight was much closer, and Parry
could see the shooting flames reflecting off his lance.
The head of the lance was burning brightly, red as
blood . . . as blood. . . .

"No!" Parry shrieked. He scrambled to his feet
and began to run. He ran for his life down the echo-
ing city alleys and streets. His brain was on fire with
pictures of blood . . . of blood. . . .

An ambulance . . . a stretcher . . . the gurney
rolling down the hospital corridor—*no!* He was in
the ambulance with the woman, holding so tightly
to her hand that the paramedics had to force him to
let go. The girl . . . the beautiful, beautiful girl . . .
so still, her face so white . . . the whiteness such a
contrast to the bright scarlet of the blood bubbling
in her brown hair—*no!* He mustn't remember! To
remember was to die.

Parry ran faster, but the Red Knight was closing
fast behind, and the secrets on the head of his lance
were stabbing their way into Parry's soul. The
woman . . . yes .. Elizabeth . . . so much love . . .
a wedding ring . . . she danced in his arms, and his
happiness was so strong that it filled him up and
bubbled over into laughter . . . laughter . . . they

were laughing together . . . they always laughed . . . the honeyed sound of Elizabeth's laughter—*no!*

Don't make me remember, he pleaded as he ran for his life. He felt the tip of the lance at his belly, pressing into his entrails. It burned.

Parry ran into traffic and east across Sixth Avenue, pelting past crowds of people out in the evening doing normal things like talking, walking together, coming out of movie houses, buying ice cream. Some of them snickered, but many of them didn't even bother to turn their heads as Parry ran by screaming. They saw a crazy little bum in a shapeless suit, and what's new about that in New York?

The Red Knight's thrusting lance probed deeper, deeper into Parry's entrails, spilling out the deadly secrets. They came tumbling out now, each one more terrible than the one before, crowding each other past Parry's brain, yelling, *Me! Me! Me! Look at me first! See me! Remember me!*

He remembered that night at Babbitt's. They had tickets to a play, Henry and Elizabeth. They didn't ordinarily go to bars, but they had an hour to spare before curtain, Elizabeth felt like having a white-wine spritzer. The place looked so cozy, with its hanging frosted-glass globes and its gleaming mahogany bar and all the fresh green plants and the happy socializing mob of pretty young people. So they went inside, sat at the bar, and Henry was on a roll, making Elizabeth laugh.

How he loved to make her laugh! She was so beautiful that he could scarcely believe this perfect creature was his wife, and she looked especially glorious when she laughed. She would throw her head back and her loose brown hair went tumbling over her shoulders in fragrant waves; her throat was exposed, long and white and smooth. He leaned forward and pressed his lips against Elizabeth's throat, and his beard tickled her and made her laugh even more.

The Red Knight galloped closer; he had his sword out now. Parry ran faster. There was no escape.

A man came into the bar; nobody noticed. Nobody ever noticed Edwin Malnick. They didn't even see him pull the weapon from under his coat. But the unexpected noise was suddenly deafening, the angry chatter of bullets. People screamed. They ran in frantic fear. They dived for the floor or crawled under tables. And some of them died screaming.

And Elizabeth . . . oh, God, Elizabeth. Her head exploded. Her precious bright red blood spattered across Henry's glasses; it was warm and sticky on his face. Her head fell forward onto his chest, and he could see the giant hole ripped through the base of her skull, see the brains oozing from her head. . . .

"Nooooooooooooo!" Parry screamed. "Stoooppp!" His face was wet with tears. And still the Red Knight galloped forward; Parry could hear the horse pounding behind him. The lance had pierced him, and now the sword was reaching out . . . reaching out . . . Parry turned. The Red Knight was nowhere in sight.

Parry was standing on the promenade by the East River; it was the very place where he had rescued Jack Lucas from the two delinquents who tried to set him on fire. Parry had run all the way there and his body was trembling with exhaustion and streaming with sweat. And now the Red Knight had disappeared. It was a trick; he knew it was a trick. The Red Knight was very near, only waiting for the right moment to disembowel him. There could be no defense against him. It would soon be over.

But Parry didn't intend to die without making a stand. With all of his strength, he cried out into the black night.

"Come on! Where *are* you? *Where are you?*" Sobbing with pain and rage, he dropped to his knees. ''Where are you?'' he wept. He felt very alone and very afraid.

Suddenly he saw his enemy. The Red Knight was riding straight at him, but he wasn't alone. With him were two dark figures, and dimly Parry recognized the same two boys he'd defeated for Jack—the one in the leather jacket and his friend in the windbreaker. They were being led toward him by the Red Knight, although they couldn't see him or hear him. Only Parry could.

Parry stood his ground. He rose up from his knees and took a few steps forward to meet his fate, on his feet. The Red Knight urged the boys on, and flames poured out of his helmet. The boys held open switchblade knives, and Parry could see the fires reflecting off the steel blades.

''We're tired of looking at you people,'' the boy in the leather jacket snarled. He slashed at Parry's defenseless chest, cutting it open. And the Red Knight's sword bit deep.

With a strangled scream, Parry fell to the ground and lay still. And then the three of them were on him—the two boys and the evil Red Knight. His enemy had him at last.

Anne came out of the bathroom, rosy from her shower, with a broad smile on her face. She hadn't felt this good in a very long time; she felt satisfied all over and well loved, inside and out. Jack had been so wonderful last night, not only passionate, but affectionate, too. Usually, whenever they made love, Jack turned away from Anne soon after his climax, to sleep alone on his side of the bed. Last night, he'd been there for her, holding her in his arms, kissing and cuddling her until they made love again. And again. Her lover loved her. What woman could ask for more?

Jack was on the telephone when Anne came into the

room in her bathrobe. He sounded very up and positive, sitting on the floor surrounded by piles of tapes from his radio show. Coming up behind him, Anne threw her arms around him in a joyous affectionate hug.

"Well, y'know, I'm feeling good, Lou, I don't know how else to put it," Jack was saying. "I had some personal problems to work out, and I have, and . . . Yeah, right . . . well, the thing is, I want to work again, Lou. I want to get back into it. You think that's possible?"

Get back to work? Anne grinned happily. This was the first she'd heard of it. Things were going great, almost *too* great; she crossed her fingers superstitiously.

"I understand, Lou." His voice was more subdued now, but Jack still sounded hopeful. "I am . . . I won't . . . I will. *Great!* When? Tuesday's great, Lou. I'll see you then. Thanks a lot, Lou." He hung up the phone, smiling.

"So, what's going on? Who's Lou?"

"Lou Rosen's my agent. I called my agent."

Anne gave a little gasp of delight. "You're kidding! What did he say?"

Jack looked very pleased with himself. "He says if I want to get back to work, I just come in. No problem. Just come in and talk, and that's it!"

"Oh, honey, that's terrific!" Anne grabbed him in a bear hug, but Jack pulled away.

"I've got to put these tapes in some kind of order, and, oh, have you seen my good jacket?"

"It's in the bedroom closet."

"Oh, yeah, there's coffee if you want."

Anne let out a joyously incredulous whoop. *"You* made coffee? You're going back to work *and* you made coffee? I love this!"

Pouring herself a cup, she sat at the little dining table watching Jack moving around so full of energy and purpose. For the first time since she met him Anne allowed herself the luxury of thinking about the future. When she had lived with Jack the self-absorbed drunk, any thought of a future was ludicrous, a pipe dream. But now things had turned one hundred and eighty degrees. Jack was staying away from the bottle and doing the right thing. Now he had phoned his agent and was even going back to work. He was her lover again, more passionate than ever before. He was her man. Anne's nesting instinct began to kick in. Life with Jack was going to be great!

"It's wonderful to see you like this, honey. I can't tell you!"

Jack had located his good Armani jacket and was going over it with a critical eye and a brush. "Thanks."

Anne took another sip from her mug. "Y'know, I'm just thinkin' . . . with two incomes coming in, I would love to look for a larger place."

Jack's hand stopped, midway up the left sleeve.

". . . I don't want to rush things, but I'd love to start looking, at least." Her eyes sparkled with pleasure at the thought of making a real home for her and Jack. "You know, maybe a two-bedroom . . . or even, maybe the top floor of a house. Like in Brooklyn"—no, Jack Lucas was definitely not the Brooklyn type.—"Heights," she finished. Brooklyn Heights was one of the most desirable, expensive, and fashionable of New York's neighborhoods, almost an adjunct of Manhattan. She glanced at Jack, hoping for his approval of her plan.

But Jack was only looking back at her, saying nothing.

"What? You don't want to commute?"

"No, it's not that." Jack shook his head. "C'mere." He took Anne into his arms, holding her against him, her back against his belly.

"You're an incredible woman—" he began, but Anne pulled herself out of his arms and looked at him sharply. "What?" he asked.

" 'I'm an incredible woman'?" Anne's voice was angry and filled with suspicion. "What is this, a death sentence?"

Oh, Jesus, she was too fuckin' smart. She had senses like a jungle cat. "I want to talk about this," Jack said. "Listen . . . so much has happened . . . and I think it would be a good thing for both of us if we slowed down a little—"

"Slowed *down?*" Anne's voice rose to a shrill pitch. "Where have I been? Have we been going fast?"

Jack bit his lip. This was not going as well as he'd hoped. "Right now I'm just not sure about . . . making definite plans."

Anne's eyes searched for Jack's, but they evaded her. "I'm lost. What are you saying?"

Oh, fuck, Jack thought miserably. She wasn't going to let him make this easy. She wasn't going to let him get away with jackshit. He should have known. Taking Anne's hand in his, Jack led her over to the sofa, and they sat down. "Look," he began gently, "it's been a real . . . difficult time for me . . . and now, for the first time in a long time, Anne, I feel like I'm above water. I feel like I know a lot more than I did, and I don't want to make any mistakes. So . . . I think I need some time . . . to make the right choices—"

"Wait! Wait!" Anne cried. "I'm lost here. What are you saying?"

"I'm saying I . . . should be alone for a while. Now that I know more, I feel that I should focus on my career. Parry's taken care of, and like I said, I know more now, and—"

Anne leaped to her feet to interrupt, her face a mask of outrage and pain. "First of all, let me tell you something! *You* don't know *shit!* Secondly, as far as *we* go, what the hell have we been doing here, except *time?* Have I ever . . . ever pressured you?" she demanded. "Once? Ever?"

"No," Jack admitted. It wasn't true, of course, she'd put plenty of pressure on him, but Anne sincerely believed she hadn't, and he had to concede that much. He didn't want to fight; above all, he didn't want to fight.

"No." Anne nodded her head. "So what time do you need, baby?" she pleaded. "I love you, you love me, you want to get your career going—I think that's the greatest thing in the world. I wanna be there. Shoot me, but I wanna be there when it happens. So what do you need time to figure out alone?"

Jack didn't speak, but he sighed deeply, and the guilty look on his face told Anne everything she needed to know. He was dumping her. With only one foot on the ladder of his old career, he couldn't wait to dump her. She'd been down this road before, and she knew all the milestones and signposts.

"All right," Anne said quietly. "So let me ask you one thing." She took in a deep breath, summoned up every ounce of strength she could command, and asked, "Do you love me?"

Jack hesitated, then: "I don't know," he confessed.

You don't know? A short bark of hysterical laughter escaped her lips. "Jesus, Jack, you can't even give me *that?* What were you gonna do? Just walk out that door, move in by yourself, and then what? Drop the news when you find somebody new? What the hell were you planning to do, Jack?" She threw back her head, challenging him to meet her eyes, to tell her the whole God's honest truth.

Jack shook his head numbly. "I don't know. I just said all I want is some time," he lied.

He was feeling even worse than he'd imagined he would. He could see how badly he was hurting Anne, but there seemed to be little he could do about it. She'd been so good to him, but Anne Napolitano was . . . wrong . . . for his new life. She didn't have enough . . . hipness and class. He was impatient to leave her behind, along with Parry and everything else that embarrassed him, all the encumbrances that he no longer had room for. Excess baggage.

"Bullshit!" Anne yelled. She was furious now, and fighting hard to keep from crying. "If you're going to hurt me, hurt me now! Not some long-drawn-out hurt that takes months of my life because you don't have the balls!"

"Okay." Jack shrugged. "I'll pack my stuff tonight."

But Anne wasn't going to let him go so easily. She knew she'd been manipulated by Jack into being the one to throw him out, just so he could ease his guilty conscience. Just as he'd used her, manipulated her all along. "What have you been doing here?" she shrieked at him. "Could you just tell me that? I wanna know. *What have you been doing here?"*

Now it was Jack Lucas's turn to show temper. He'd been trying to avoid a fight, but Anne was pressing all his guilt buttons, and he didn't like it. What she was accusing him of was cutting pretty close to the bone. "Listen!" he yelled back. "We both got something out of it, all right?"

This was too much for Anne. "Oh, yeah? What did I get?" she demanded. "What did I get I couldn't have gotten from somebody with no name any night of the week? You think your company is such a treat? Your moods, your 'pain' . . ." She threw the words in his teeth with heavy sarcasm. "Your problems? You think this has been entertaining for me?"

"Then what do you want to stay with me for?"

The stupidity, the insensitivity of the question drove Anne Napolitano over the edge, and she lost the control she'd been fighting so hard to hold on to. Darting forward, her hands forming into fists, she attacked Jack, hitting him everywhere she could reach—his head, his face, his chest and shoulders. And the tears streamed down her face.

"Because I love you!" she yelled, trying to make him understand, trying to force comprehension into

him. *"You stupid . . . fuckin' . . . because I love you!"*

Jack blocked her blows as best he could, finally pinning her arms to her sides. Loud sobs escaped her, and she almost fell. Jack found his heart aching with pity, and he attempted to embrace her, to kiss her wet cheeks, whispering softly, "Anne, Anne, hey, it's gonna be okay, shhhhh."

But Anne would have none of his pity or embraces. She was too proud to sell herself so cheaply, for such tiny rewards. She'd been used enough already, and the only excuse she could make to herself was that she thought Jack loved her. But he didn't; he never had. Anne felt so damn dumb for not having realized it before. She pulled away from him.

"No, no, you don't get to be nice now. I'm not gonna play some stupid game with you where we act like friends so you can walk out that door feeling good about yourself. I'm not a modern woman. If it's over, then let's just call it over."

Jack felt a sudden pang of disappointment, even loss. Life totally without Anne . . . he hadn't thought about that . . . what if they . . . ?

The telephone rang. For the space of a couple of heartbeats, they stood looking at it as though it were an alien thing. Then Jack picked up the receiver.

"Hello? Yeah?" His face looked puzzled. "My wallet? What do you mean?" There was a sharp intake of breath, and Anne looked at him. Jack looked terrible. What was going on?

"What? When?" Jack exclaimed sharply. He listened a minute, then hung up the phone, turning to Anne.

"It's Parry," he said in a low voice, and his face was ashen with fear.

"Oh, Jesus," Anne whispered.

Seventeen

Jack Lucas had never seen anybody who wasn't dead lying so still. It didn't appear as though there was any spark of life in Parry. Bandaged tightly across the chest, both arms in a cast, a thick bandage wrapped around his head, he lay on his hospital bed with his eyes open, not seeing, not hearing. Under his beard, Parry's face was as white as the bandages. There was no flicker of the eyelid, no intake of breath. Yet he didn't look dead, he appeared merely to have . . . gone away.

"Parry?" Jack called softly. He stood at the foot of Parry's ward bed with Anne behind him. As soon as Anne had gotten dressed, they'd rushed over to the hospital. In the taxi Jack told her what little he knew from the telephone call. Parry had been attacked by homicidal muggers, slashed in the chest, and beaten very badly. Both his arms were broken, and he had suffered a head wound. He was alive, but only barely. And he'd lapsed into a coma. The doctors weren't hopeful.

Parry's attackers hadn't bothered to check his pockets for money; what would a homeless bum be doing with money? So when he was brought into the hospital, the ER attendant found Jack Lucas's wallet still tucked safely in the jacket pocket of the slashed and bloody Versace suit and, using it for identification, had tracked Jack Lucas down.

"Parry?" he called again.

"He can't hear you," a voice said behind them. Anne and Jack turned. A middle-aged doctor, his face weary from lack of sleep, his eyes red-rimmed and pouchy with fatigue, was coming into the ward carrying a chart.

"Hi, I'm Dr. Mandeville." He shook hands with them both. "I was on duty when they brought him in. I've been going over his record. He was brought in once before, I understand."

Flipping open the thick chart, Dr. Mandeville read out loud from it. " 'Catatonic stupor' . . . hmmm . . . 'condition rendered him nonverbal for a period of—' "

"Yeah, so?" Jack interrupted defensively. That was then; this is now. "The guy's been beat up. He . . . he probably has a concussion or something, right? He's gonna snap out of it?"

Dr. Mandeville shook his head, frowning. "I'm afraid not. The beating's bad, but that's not the problem. It seems he's reexperiencing the catatonia. So, like before, he could snap out of it in an hour, or in thirteen months, or in thirteen years . . . I don't know. There's no way to be sure."

"But how could that happen?" Jack wanted to know. He looked at Parry again, trying to detect some flicker of movement—an eyelid, something! Nothing.

The physician shrugged. "A person could actually reexperience the full effect of a tragedy long after the event took place. I was reading how he lost his wife. Are you relatives?" He looked sharply at Jack and Anne.

Jack shook his head and Anne said nothing.

"Well, it doesn't matter," Dr. Mandeville said in a resigned voice. "We'll take care of it. He'll have to be sent back to the same institution." He riffled through the chart, looking for the name and address of Parry's former mental hospital.

"What if I was a relative?" Jack asked suddenly, his voice thick.

"Well, you'd have the option of caring for him at home, but I wouldn't recommend it. He needs hospital care. I just thought you could sign the release forms, but the city can do that."

Dr. Mandeville didn't mean to be brusque, but there was really nothing more he could tell them, and more than two dozen patients he still had to see. Besides, there was nothing anybody could do for a case like this one, and the mental-hospital wards were overflowing with the schizophrenic homeless, so the doctor moved on.

For a long moment Jack and Anne looked down at the small bandaged figure on the hospital bed. Then Anne said, with a bitter smile, "Poor Lydia. She finally finds her prince, and he falls into a coma." She raised one eyebrow at Jack. "Some women just have all the luck, huh?"

She turned, and with enormous dignity and renewed self-respect, she walked out of the ward and out of Jack Lucas's life.

"Anne, Anne, I'll call you, okay?" Jack called after her. But she didn't answer, didn't stop, and didn't look back.

Jack turned again to stare at Parry. Great, now they were back to Square One. Nothing that Jack had done for Parry counted now; he might as well have thrown his efforts into the crapper and flushed. Parry was gone beyond anybody's help, reliving the original nightmare that was Jack Lucas's making. Anger, guilt, and frustration tore at Jack, but he refused to give in to them. This isn't my fault, he raged at Parry silently. I'm not to blame. My intentions were good. And it worked, didn't it? You wanted Lydia, God only knows why, and I had handed her over to you on a silver platter. So I'm off the hook now. You can't raise the damn ante on me anymore. We're even. I'm getting my old life back, and there won't be time enough or room enough in it for you. Besides, you don't need me anymore. You don't need anybody anymore. So I'm taking off. Good-bye.

But Parry couldn't see him, hear him or speak to him, and Jack Lucas felt like shit.

"Well, I'm gone. Have a perfect weekend, and remember, if you've often wondered, 'What *is* sodomy exactly?' well, you're in luck. Monday's special studio guest is an expert on the subject. It's Ben Starr, star of the recently defunct hit TV show *On the Radio,* and he'll have the answer to that question and many more when he tells us exactly how and why he was busted in an Atlanta airport men's room. Be sure to tune us in on Monday, and until then, from one of the Botched to all you Bungled cats out there, I love ya, and right back atcha! So long." The theme music "Hit the Road, Jack" swelled up and out and Jack cut a switch. Off the air. Thank God.

Rubbing at his tired eyes with the heels of his hands, he slumped into his seat at the control board. Back on the air six months now, and he still couldn't get used to the grind. Something had gone out of the work—the thrill of power, maybe—Jack wasn't sure. All he knew was that in the old days he had a hard-on for his voice on the air, and now he just didn't seem to give much of a damn. And he no longer saw any percentage in making fun of the weirdos who called in. He let them describe their fantasies without much interruption. Who was he to pass judgment? Even the gleeful satisfaction he would have felt in the past for the downfall of the very TV actor he most envied was tempered by his ennui, by a feeling of "what does it all mean, anyway? Nothing, nothing at all."

The telephone rang in the studio, Jack's private line. Wearily, he picked it up. "Yeah? Yeah, Lou."

He listened for a minute, his face darkening like a thundercloud, then cut in angrily. "Lou, I said I want a firm offer or they can forget it. Well, you tell them I'm meeting with the cable people about a talk show and . . . what? Beth's father set it up. . . . No, he owns it. Yeah, yeah . . . fuck you, Lou. If the network is ready to make a firm offer and they want to send a script, then fine. Otherwise, forget it. . . . All right, see you then."

He hung up. He should get up now and go home to his luxurious new Tribeca loft with its sweeping views of the Great South Bay and the Statue of Liberty. Beth would already be waiting there for him, all sleek perfect blondness with long waxed legs and a flexible body, and a father who had the bucks and the clout to turn Jack Lucas into a superstar. They'd make love, eat a salad with a glass of wine, and get ready for the long drive out to Southampton for a weekend of opulence and sailing with Beth's folks. Yes, he really did have to get up now. He hadn't packed yet for the weekend. His crew of engineers had already gone home. His girlfriend was waiting. A whole new life was waiting.

But Jack Lucas still sat alone in the darkened studio, his hands cupped tightly against his eyes.

The network people didn't have the final script ready for Jack to see, but they were very eager to meet with him and "give him a feel for it," as the production exec told Lou Rosen. It was a "high concept" show, whatever the hell that meant, a comedy, and they wanted Jack Lucas's input.

Grudgingly, Jack donned his new Yohji Yamamoto jacket, stuck his feet into his latest snakeskin cowboy boots, put his Vuarnet shades on his nose, and took in the meeting. He and his agent limoed over to the sixty-seven-story black glass-and-steel office skyscraper that housed the network and dominated its corner of Fortieth Street and Park Avenue. When the two men stepped out of the limousine, a minor scuffle was going on outside the main entrance, on the stepped plaza that led to the doors. A security guard was chasing away a panhandler. Just another crummy New York scene, like a million others. Jack paid no attention as he stalked past the fountains on the plaza, but then he heard his name being yelled.

"Jack! Jack! It's *meee!* Remember me? I have to talk to you! Jack!"

He turned. The panhandler was Michael, the little gay man he'd found with Parry on the bridle path in Central Park, the one who'd sung his heart out in the medley from *Gypsy* to a stunned Lydia Sinclair.

Before Jack could say anything, the security guard had reached Michael and was grabbing him, pushing him away roughly. Next to the guard's uniformed beefiness, Michael looked puny and fragile.

"Get outta here, I said!" roared the guard.

Lou Rosen grabbed Jack by the arm and tried to hustle him into the building, but Jack half turned back, uncertain of what to do. The guard had his billy out now and was poking Michael in the side with it. Every poke drove him a few feet farther away, but Michael continued to bawl out to Jack.

"Jack! Please, you know me! Please, can I talk to you?" He stretched out a pitifully thin arm. "Please . . . please!!"

Suddenly Jack became aware that people were staring at him, connecting him with this pathetic bum. That decided him. Hiding behind his sunglasses, he ducked his head and followed Lou into the network building. Behind him, he could hear Michael's screams dying away, hoarse and desperate.

"Jack! Please, Jaaaack! Why won't anybody talk to me? Leave me alone! Don't hurt me! Leave me alone! Jaaaackkkkk!!"

* * *

"It's a weekly comedy about the homeless," announced the network exec. sounding very pleased with himself. "But it's not depressing in any way."

Jack made an effort not to let his expression change, but he couldn't believe what he was hearing! This pompous asshole was pitching him the single worst, most tasteless, most denigrating and inhuman idea Jack Lucas had ever heard. A comedy about the homeless?

Jack looked around the executive's huge office, furnished in Italian Modern—all polished surfaces like marble and steel—and heavy fabrics by Donghia. This dickhead got paid to think up shit like this? On the ammonite marble coffee table in front of the black leather sofa was a stack of the latest glossy magazines. On top, a copy of *World Weekly*, with its cover story—"Billionaire Langdon Carmichael buys Vincent Van Gogh's *Road with Cypresses* for $20 Million."

What a fucking insane world this is, Jack thought bitterly. Some poor schmuck with a burning genius in his gut is driven insane by manic-depression and the compulsion to paint. Everybody except his brother hates what he paints, and in his whole lifetime he sells only one picture. So he puts a bullet into his brain in a madhouse before he's forty. And today, a real-estate baron buys one of his paintings for enough money to support a third-world country for years. Only the poor schmuck painter, the mad genius, has been dead for a hundred years and will never know that, all along, he was right and everybody else was wrong.

The TV guy was now warming to his pitch. "We want to find a funny, upbeat way of bringing the issue of homelessness to television. So we've got three wacky homeless characters, but they're wise. They're wacky and they're wise. And the hook is"—and here the exec's oily voice sounded more pleased with itself than ever—"they *love* being homeless. They love the freedom . . . they love the adventure. It's about the joy of living, not all the bullshit *we* have to deal with—the money, the politics, the pressures. And the best part is . . ." The exec paused for maximum timing, for the brilliance of the punch line. "The best part is, it's called *Home Free.*"

Finished with his masterly presentation at last, the network honcho looked to the others for their reaction.

"Oooohhh, I'm getting a rush," said Lou Rosen dutifully. He knew how to earn his fifteen percent.

Jack Lucas wanted to vomit. He stood up suddenly, and without a word, he bolted out of the room.

The executive's jaw dropped and his brows drew together in a scowl. "What the fuck . . . ? Where the hell is he going? Lou, is this another disappearing act with this guy or what?"

"Not a problem," Rosen assured him hastily. "Just a bathroom break. I'll check. . . ." And he hurried out in search of Jack.

Jack got an express elevator and was down in the lobby in a matter of forty seconds. He raced out the entrance to the plaza and looked around for Michael, but the little guy was gone, pushed off the edge of the world by security with a badge and a billy club. Shoving his hands deep into the pockets of his criminally expensive jacket, Jack walked quickly away from the network building. His belly churned in disgust. Disgust for the television world and their tasteless sitcoms, disgust for the values of a so-called society that places money above humanity. Most of all, disgust for himself because he bought into the scam, and because he was now beginning to suspect that his own value system consisted of the fact that Jack Lucas had no values.

Eighteen

For six months, ever since they'd moved Parry to Oakbrook Institute, the mental hospital on Staten Island, nobody had lived in the boiler room. There was a heavy layer of dust and soot over everything, but the room was otherwise kept just as Parry had left it. Frank the superintendent had seen to that. Jack came in, closed the door behind him, and looked around the place.

There sat little Pinocchio, still standing guard, his wooden arms straight out like a soldier presenting his rifle, his painted eyes watching without fatigue.

Funny, a lot of Parry's stuff made a kind of sense to Jack now. At least, he understood its significance somewhat better, because he understood Parry somewhat better. Curiously, he examined the strange handmade weapons that Parry had used. He unfolded again the map of Langdon Carmichael's armory and studied it. He saw that Parry had gotten ropes and grappling hooks ready, as though they were actually going to break into the burglar-proof armory. The nut! There was just no convincing him. Deeply depressed, Jack sat down at the small table and tried to put it all together in his mind. He attempted to see through Parry's eyes.

Henry Sagan, historian, thinking man, man of reason and intellect and humanity and goodness, had been dealt the most cruel and sudden blow. Everything he cherished most in the world had been torn to pieces before his eyes, in a split second, and there'd been nothing he could do to prevent it. He'd seen his wife's brains blown out, and he hadn't been able to lift a finger.

What had gone through his mind? First, shock, and then denial, and then an incurable grief. A human life snuffed out in an instant. And not just any human life, but the life most precious and most necessary to Henry's happiness. No, it couldn't be! Denial. Thwarted rage—the killer had taken his own life. Guilt, because Henry Sagan was still alive, while his innocent wife was senselessly dead. All these intense emotions, and all of them boiling through his brain at the same time. Enough negative input to stun an elephant, and surely enough to kill a vulnerable human being.

But the human mind is a strange and wonderful organ. It moves to protect itself, whether the person owning it wants to be protected or not. When an electrical circuit is overloaded, a fuse blows or a circuit-breaker switch throws itself. The power is thereby shut off. The deadly overload in Henry Sagan's brain did much the same thing—it threw his circuits into catatonia so that he wouldn't have to remember or deal with the powerful memories of those terrible events. Catatonia, a state in which electrical activity in the brain is at an absolute minimum. To protect itself, Henry Sagan's brain had shut itself off.

For thirteen months after that night at Babbitt's, Henry Sagan had lain in a hospital bed, not seeing, not speaking, not moving, a catatonic. Yet underneath the stillness, under all the rejection of sensory stimuli, a rather wonderful thing was taking place. Just as a coral reef is carefully built up of organisms too tiny to be seen by the naked eye, all accreting into a living growth of wondrous complex beauty, so Henry Sagan's brain began slowly to heal itself, to turn the power back on, a few volts at a time. His unconscious mind worked to select the necessary elements to construct the intricate coral reef of his new identity.

Out of the pieces of his old life, Henry's sleeping mind chose the mystical elements of the medieval time he knew and loved so much. The focus of his delusion would become the Holy Grail, because, deep in his soul, he was aware that the Grail, if achieved, had the power to heal. It is only the Holy Grail—Christian symbol of God's grace—that could cure the incurable wound from which Henry suffered so deep a pain.

And who can achieve the Grail? Only the One who is pure in thought and deed. Who achieved it in Henry's researches into the legend of the Fisher King? The fool, because a childlike fool is pure, simple, sacred to God. And because only the fool could see what was hidden from the sight of other men. So to the beautiful growing organism in Henry Sagan's catatonic mind the vital element of God's fool was added. In Arthurian legend, Sir Galahad had the strength of ten and won the Holy Grail. Sir Percival, with but the strength of one, was vouchsafed a vision of the sacred chalice, and thus was granted God's grace. Percival, also known as Parsifal. Parsifal . . . Parry.

Jesus! The sudden piecing together of this set of cryptic clues brought an illumination that surprised Jack greatly, yet it possessed a certain kind of logic, if he put a sideways spin on the logic.

After thirteen months in the dark, Parry had opened his eyes. He was insane because his brain knew that insanity would be his protection. He had become the childlike fool with the clear vision. Hallucinations of floating cherubim dispatched Parry upon a quest, to achieve God's grace and healing. But to do that he needed a Galahad. Parry was alone, with the strength of one. He needed the strength of ten. Oh shit, Jack thought, *me*. I'm supposed to be fuckin' Sir Galahad. Isn't that a laugh and a half? Pure Jack Lucas, undefiled, untainted, chivalrous, saintly Jack Lucas. That's how Parry perceived him. Jack didn't know whether to laugh or to cry.

Keep going. Every knight deserves a lady, a damsel in distress. Enter Lydia Sinclair. Something deep inside Parry, some atavistic memory of Henry Sagan, buried deep, told Parry that he didn't dare again to court beauty. Beauty was too dangerously tempting to destroyers and much too easily destroyed. He needed someone made of stronger, more common clay. So he picked out of millions one awkward, homely girl and invested her with the beauty and grace of his fantasy, and he elevated her above all other women. To be his lady fair.

Every knight must fight his dragons. And dragons are evil, spewing forth fire, snatching life and breath away with choking fumes, cruel sharp teeth, and greedy reptilian fingers. They fly swiftly on leather wings and defile whatever they touch, with their smoky breath and scarlet claws. Jack got up, walked over to the wall, and studied the poster of the Red Knight.

For the first time he could recognize that it was flames Parry had scribbled with his crimson Magic Marker. He saw that the Red Knight personified the dragon nemesis, the guardian of everything evil, the enemy that placed itself between the questing knight and the Holy Grail. The Red Knight was the perilous dragon that Parry had to slay. It was a terrible vision he saw.

So this hodgepodge of a room, this unholy mess, actually represented a complex but unmistakably unified private universe. Parry could see it; now Jack caught a glimpse of it, too. And it scared him—the logic of it, the magnetic power of it, scared him.

And what frightened Jack Lucas the most was the overwhelming need that a small crazy man named Parry had for the healing power of the Holy Grail.

Jack paid off the taxi and stood looking at the grounds of the Oakbrook Institute. It had taken him an hour and a half and sixty-five bucks plus tip to get out here to the other end of Staten Island; traffic on the Verrazano Bridge was a nightmare. It seemed like an okay place, nothing special, but nothing too depressing about it. Low brick buildings, built sometime in the 1950s, with bars on the windows. Patients in bathrobes sitting on benches taking the air while other patients were wandering aimlessly or pacing nervously around the grounds. Burly men and woman in white uniforms keeping a professional eye on them. Your average common-or-garden loony bin.

In Parry's ward, there were beds lined up on both sides of the long room. A television set was on, tuned to a channel that was showing cartoons, but nobody seemed to be watching. There were a number of torpid unshaven men crouched on their beds, their hospital gowns flapping open to reveal certain unsavory parts that were better kept covered. By contrast, Parry looked absolutely gorgeous.

He was dressed in what appeared to be brand-new pajamas, lime green, printed all over with watermelons and other fruits in bright incongruous colors. His bed was freshly and tightly made, and had sheets that no hospital had ever issued. These were colored percale, with contrasting hemstitched borders, obviously expensive, and quite beautiful. Fresh spring flowers stood in a vase by his bed.

Parry himself looked like a sleeping prince. His hair was neatly brushed and combed, his beard trimmed evenly. Apart from that, he was out of it, totally and completely out of it. Catatonic. He lay on his back with his arms folded on his chest; his eyes were closed tightly, and he didn't appear to be breathing in or out.

Jack just stood there at the foot of Parry's bed watching him while an enormous tidal wave of emotion rolled over him. Regret, mostly, but also anger, resentment, frustration, guilt. Jack had believed he could go back easily to his good life, but it hadn't worked. Oh, he had everything he wanted—the right address, good threads, a rich and thin girlfriend with an influential father, a booming career. He'd spent the last six months building up his defense mechanisms again, setting new stones and mortar into the wall around him that had been breached that night at Babbitt's. He'd built it strong, sure that this time it would stand.

But seeing Michael today—and turning his back on him like a Judas—had opened a crack in that wall. Forced to listen to that impossible asshole prattling about a homeless sitcom—"they're wacky and they're wise"—had made the crack wider. Afterward, going to Parry's little boiler room and seeing Parry's life with new eyes had blown an enormous hole in the wall, leaving Jack Lucas standing troubled in the ruins. His defenses had crumbled away. His wall had become useless.

A familiar voice outside in the corridor made Jack turn his head. An unmistakable voice, yet . . . perhaps . . . not as abrasive as he remembered. Going to the door of the ward, he looked down the hall to the nurses' station. A young woman was talking to one of the nurses. It was Lydia Sinclair.

"Pardon me, but not long ago I brought new bed sheets for him," Lydia was saying. "They were lime-colored with little watermelons on them? To match his pajamas?"

"Oh yes," the nurse replied. "I'm sorry. They're being cleaned. The doctor had a little accident with a hypo."

"I see. Please just make sure that he does get them when they *are* cleaned. Thank you."

Please? Thank you? Jack grinned in surprise. It sure didn't sound like the old Lydia. Didn't look much like the old Lydia, either. Seeing her start up the corridor, Jack ducked back quickly into the ward so she wouldn't spot him, but he managed to get a good look at her as she walked by on her way out of the hospital.

Lydia was wearing a colorful form-fitting dress that showed off her narrow waist and small rear end. Her hair was longer and brushed back softly off her face and—was it possible? Yes! She was even wearing a little makeup. Nothing heavy, but some pink blusher and matching lipstick that brought color to her face, and a little eye makeup that brought out the large size and fine hazel color of her eyes. She walked with grace and a spring in her step. She looked like . . . a woman in love.

The fancy sheets and colorful pajamas on Parry, the flowers by his bedside, his neatly brushed hair and trimmed beard—all Lydia. She was a woman with a mission now—to take good care of her man. And it had brought out all her womanliness. Gone was the old shy, suspicious, self-protective Lydia. In her place was this new, trim young woman who stepped on by with confidence, who knew what she wanted, and who, incidentally—Jack marveled—wasn't so bad to look at either. He had never noticed them in those god-awful orthopedic shoes she used to wear, but now, in midheel slingbacks, Lydia Sinclair had great legs.

He watched her leave the hospital by the front door, then turned his attention back to the ward. These were evidently the worst cases, the ones who never left their beds or walked on the grounds outside. Whacked-out on Thorazine, these hopeless men mumbled to themselves, or sat rocking themselves as though they were babies, or just stared off into space. In the middle of them was Parry, like the eye of a storm, white and still.

"Hi!" said Jack. "It's me, Jack. How are ya doing? You look good. You do."

If he expected Parry to respond, he was in for a big disappointment. But Jack came closer to the bed and picked up Parry's limp hand. He gave it a little shake. "Hey, you gonna wake up for me? Huh?" Dropping the hand, he scowled and leaned over the bed, almost nose to nose with Parry.

"This isn't over, is it?" he asked resentfully. "You think you're going to make me do this, don't you? Well, *forget it!* No fuckin' way! I don't feel responsible for you, or for anybody! Everybody has bad things happen to them. . . . I'm not God!" I don't decide. People . . . survive." Jack looked bleakly at Parry. *"Say something!"*

But Parry gave no sign that he could see or hear. Furiously, Jack began to pace up and down near the bed, arguing more at himself than for Parry's unconscious benefit. "Everything's been going great. *Great!* I'm gonna have my own cable talk show, with an incredible equity, I might add. I . . . I have an incredibly fucking gorgeous girlfriend. . . . I am living an *incredibly fucking life!* So don't lay there in your comfortable little coma, and think I'm going to risk all of that because I feel responsible for you!"

Jack glared around at the other patients as though they were judge and jury. *"I am not responsible!"* he roared.

"And I don't feel guilty," he told the unresponding Parry. "You've got it easy! I'm out there every day. Every fuckin' *day* trying to figure out what the hell I'm doing. And why, no matter what I have, it feels like I have nothing! So just don't think I feel sorry for you! It's *easy* being nuts! Try being *me!*"

Jack dragged a chair up to Parry's bed and sat

down in it, bending over the comatose man and speaking more softly but very intensely. He was bitterly angry.

"So I won't do it. I don't believe in this shit. And don't give me that stuff about me being the One! There is *nothing* . . . nothing special about me! *I* control my own destiny . . . *me!* . . . not some floating overweight fairies. *I* decide what I'm going to do, and I am *not* risking my life to get some *fucking* cup for some *fucking vegetable.* . . ."

Hurling himself out of the chair, Jack knocked it over on its side. "Motherfucker!" he raged in his despair. "What am I supposed to do? What am I supposed to do?" And in a desperate whisper, "What am I supposed to *do?*"

He turned back to Parry. "Okay," he said in a calmer voice, "suppose for the sake of argument I *did* do this. I want you to know it wouldn't be because I had to! It wouldn't be because I feel guilty or cursed . . . or . . . responsible . . . or anything." He began to weep gently, tears filling his eyes and spilling over down his cheeks. "If I do this—and I mean *if!*—it's because *I* want to do this . . . for *you.* That's all! For you!"

Jack bent over the bed, looking deeply into Parry's sleeping face. His tears fell onto Parry's cheeks, wetting them, but Parry didn't move or open his eyes. He kissed the unconscious man gently on the forehead. "Don't go anywhere, huh?" Jack Lucas whispered. "I'll be back."

Nineteen

At this minute Jack Lucas ought to have been sitting in front of a log fire crackling brightly in a big stone fireplace in a three-million-dollar dune house in Southampton, a drink in his hand, a willowy adoring blonde at his side, a day of sailing behind him. Instead of which, Jack, looking like the King of the Idiots and feeling even dumber, was standing in front of Langdon Carmichael's armory on Fifth Avenue at midnight. And there went the fucking weekend. Shit, shit, and double shit.

Only a fool would go on a quest for the Holy Grail; the catch was, only a fool would find it. To find his own salvation, a man must first find the fool locked inside himself and set it free. Jack knew instinctively that to carry out Parry's plan, he'd have to do it Parry's way. The hard way.

So back he went to the boiler room, pocketed the plan of the armory from Parry's table, tore out the page from the glossy magazine that showed Carmichael standing in front of the bookcase with the Grail, and collected the ropes and hooks and other primeval, low-tech no-tech burglary tools that Mr. Camelot had assembled for this lunatic escapade. On the way out, almost as an afterthought, Jack had taken Parry's ragged old blanket cloak and Parry's little spangled hat, too. Now, heaven alone knew why, because Jack Lucas certainly didn't, he was actually dressed in them, looking like a refugee from a cheap school production of *Arthur and His Knights*. Sir Galahad . . . only in your worst nightmare.

Wonderful. Jack was about to break into a famous billionaire's home that was equipped with every known security device except pit bulls. Shit, maybe there *were* pit bulls. And he was going to do it with his bare hands, a hook, and a piece of old rope. Step right up, world, come one, come all, see Jack Lucas make a fucking ass of himself and maybe get killed in the bargain. Well, why not? The weekend was shot anyhow.

He looked around. By the light of the corner street lamp, this stretch of Fifth Avenue was deserted. Across the street were the dark reaches of Central Park; nobody went in there at this time of night. Nobody who expected to come out again, that is. Jack tested the grappling hook, making certain it was attached firmly to the rope. Okay. He might be no Boy Scout, but it seemed to Jack the knots would probably hold a man of his size and weight.

Taking a few steps back, Jack whirled the rope around like a cowboy's lariat and let the end with the grappling hook go, hoping to catch the hook behind one of the roof's crenellations. It flew through the air, hit the building, and bounced back to the ground, a good ten feet short of the mark. Try again. And again. Each time the hook slammed into the ground, it sounded like a car crash. Yet nobody came. Nobody called the cops. What do you expect? New York. Nobody gives a shit.

His arms starting to ache, Jack heaved the hook again. This time, by some miracle, it landed on the roof of the armory and caught behind one of the crenellations. Son of a bitch, what do you know? Now for the hard part, actually climbing the thing. Since he'd stopped drinking so much, Jack Lucas was more fit than he'd been in years, but climbing up a three-story building on a rope was something else again. For that you needed to be more than fit; you needed to be nuts.

"Shit," Jack muttered when he was four feet off the ground. At six feet, he groaned, and he kept groaning as he made his way inch by tortured inch up the stone wall of the armory toward the roof. His arms felt as though they were tearing loose of their sockets. His chest ached and his breath came rasping through his lips. *If I live through this, I have to give up smoking.* All his weight—and Jack stood a couple of muscular inches over six feet—was being supported on an ordinary rope and on the strength in his hands and arms. The higher off the ground he got, the harder it was not to look down. But Jack knew he didn't dare look down.

What could possibly happen? For one thing, the damn rope could break; it was just a piece of crap that Parry had no doubt picked up out of some garbage pile. Or the grappling hook could tear loose of the stone. In either case, Jack would go plunging down twenty-five or thirty feet to a messy splatter the sidewalk, no doubt screaming his fucking lungs out all the way down.

Or the cops could come. Stranger things had happened, even in New York City. They could be cruising by in a patrol car, eyes peeled for trouble in the neighborhood—naaahhh. "Thank God I live in a city where no one looks up," Jack muttered, gritting his teeth and sweating.

He reached the roof at last, but he was still hanging underneath it, the parapet above his head. He was going to have to swing up and over the parapet. He'd seen it done a thousand times in a thousand costume pictures. Up with the legs and over. C'mon, Jack, up and over. You can do it, come on! Easier grunted than done.

There was a noise off in the distance and Jack hung there, hands blistering on the rope, heart thudding in his chest, just frozen, listening. Horses? He could swear he heard the pounding of hooves. Not the gentle trot of a rented saddle horse, but a pounding galloping. It sounded like one horse, one rider, both extremely heavy, as though they were carrying the weight of iron armor. The noise was coming closer . . . closer . . . Jack shut his eyes.

But there was no horse. Just as suddenly as it came, the galloping stopped. It didn't die away; it just stopped. An eerie silence hung over everything.

"Oh, great!" Jack muttered, spooked. "This is great. I'm hearing horses now. Parry will be so pleased." He pictured in his mind's eye the headline "Radio Personality Turns Screwball on Mission from God," and uttered a hollow laugh. "I just hope that when they put me away they find me a bed right next to his!" Pissed off with himself and the world, he gave himself a mighty heave, and suddenly Jack was over the parapet.

His feet hit the roof with a thud, and Jack gratefully hauled the rope up after him and worked the grappling hook free from the crenellation. Okay, that was the easy part. Now he was going to have to actually break into the house.

He knew Parry's plan by heart; there was a skylight window around the bend of the roof. It was the only way he could break in. Naturally, the skylight was wired into the alarm system; Jack would have to be very careful not to touch anything on the perimeter of the glass or the outer edges of the glass itself. The wiring on these new alarms was hair-trigger sensitive. One little finger touch in the wrong place and it would be jeez Louise, all over with.

Yes, there was the skylight, exactly where it appeared on Parry's diagram. Score one for the catatonic. Reaching under the clumsy cloak, Jack managed to get into his pocket and take out a roll of masking tape. Working swiftly, he made three big loops of the tape and pressed them against the glass, well away from the perimeter. So far, so good.

Now he got out the glass cutter and, very slowly, his heartbeat hammering in his ears, he began to cut out a pane of glass, wide enough for him to get his body through. Minutes passed; the cutting took an excruciatingly long time. It seemed like an eternity before the hole was finished, time enough for the alarm to go off, cops to come, and all hell to break loose. But nothing happened. Pressing his arm against the loops of tape, Jack lifted the pane out intact, without setting off the alarm. Hey, it worked! Even Jack was surprised; he was getting pretty good at this. Maybe there was a career in lawbreaking ahead of him.

Jack set the glass gently down on the roof, made sure the grappling hook was firmly in place against stone, and carefully lowered himself down on the rope through the opening in the skylight. Below him was a pitch-black hole; he had no way of knowing how far he had to drop. All he knew was that the rope was too short, his feet were in midair, and he was dangling in space.

He had to take the chance. Letting go of the rope, he dropped to the floor beneath him, about six feet. He landed with a grunt and a thud. Picking himself up gingerly, he felt to see that nothing was broken. Nothing was. He was inside the house; it was too dark to see exactly where, but inside. Risking discovery, Jack pulled the magazine article from his pocket and lit up his cigarette lighter. He studied the article. The Holy Grail was in the library on the first floor. He was up on the third. He'd have to get down to the library without making noise. He had no idea who might be in the house. Maybe Langdon Carmichael. Maybe the servants. Maybe guests. Maybe all of them. Still, he had no other options. He had to take the chance.

Jack made his way cautiously toward the broad curving staircase up ahead. But a movement in the shadows stopped him dead in his tracks. He felt a chill prickling his skin. He wasn't alone. Somebody or something was there, and was moving forward, straight at him. There, where the landing met the top of the stairs. As Jack's eyes adjusted to the darkness he could see it was a human figure.

The figure stepped out of the shadows. Jack Lucas gasped in horror and disbelief.

It was Edwin Malnick, and in his hands was a shotgun.

Jack stood paralyzed with fear, watching Edwin Malnick raise the shotgun and cock it, aiming straight for Jack's chest. His finger touched the trigger. Jack closed his eyes.

The deafening noise of the shotgun blast resonated through Jack's brain. It echoed down the hallways as it must have echoed that night in Babbitt's. In his mind, for the first time Jack could actually hear the screams of those poor terrified doomed people who'd come in for a drink and found death instead. For the first time he *was* one of those people.

He opened his eyes. He was alive. There was no wound in his chest, no blood on his shirt, no blood on the floor, and no Edwin Malnick. And Jack Lucas realized that Edwin Malnick had been his own Red Knight, and that he had inevitably to meet him face-to-face and experience for himself that grisly scene he'd always managed to evade.

Somehow, although he was shaky, Jack felt stronger now. He walked quietly down the stairs to the library, keeping a sharp eye out for the small red electric-eye lights of the electronic surveillance cameras. On the walls of the staircase hung the famous Langdon Carmichael art purchases—the Monet, the Picassos, and now the magnificent new twenty-million-dollar Van Gogh. Jack couldn't take the time to appreciate them. He entered the library. The house was very still; it appeared that nobody was home, not even the servants. This might be easier than Jack had dared hope for.

The library was a huge room, far more impressive than it appeared in the magazine photographs, its walls totally lined with books, and with very high ceilings and a baronial fireplace at the far end. A green leather high-backed chair was drawn up near the fireplace, in which a fire was burning, and a small lamp was lighted on a table next to the chair. The light from the lamp fell directly on the bookcase, illuminating it. On the shelves were the precious objects that Carmichael collected, priceless manuscripts, a Degas bronze, some Cellini gold, and . . . the Holy Grail.

It was incredible. There, on the second shelf of the bookcase, stood a beautiful silver chalice. Jack opened the cabinet and took the Grail reverently into his hands. There was some writing on it. He turned it over in his hands and read the words inscribed in the silver.

o Little Lannie Carmichael for All His Hard Work
P.S. 247 Christmas Pageant 1932''

Jack smiled. A commemorative loving cup; he should have guessed. Just a treasured souvenir of long ago, nothing mystical or magic about it. Even so, although it might not be *the* Grail, it was Parry's Grail, and he'd take it anyhow. It was what he'd come for. Tucking it under his arm, he turned to go.

That's when Jack noticed something for the first time. Somebody was slumped in the high-backed chair in front of the fireplace. A man, dressed only in expensive silk pajamas and an elegant robe. Jack took a backward step, but the man didn't move. He appeared to be asleep. Then Jack saw the rest of the picture. The empty bottle of Stolichnaya vodka on the table, the overturned glass. And, on the floor, lay an uncapped pill bottle, all the pills gone.

Kneeling swiftly, Jack checked the pharmacist's label on the bottle. It was made out to Langdon Carmichael, and it was Seconal, a powerful barbiturate. A suicide. Was it over, or had Jack interrupted it? He put down the chalice, reached around Carmichael's neck and tried to find an arterial pulse with his fingers. Nothing . . . no, wait . . . yes, there was the faintest pulse. Jack put his hand on the man's chest and could feel a heartbeat that was barely there. Langdon Carmichael was still alive, but only just.

Christ, what should he do? It was evident that Carmichael had sent all the servants away for the evening in order to have the privacy to kill himself. There was nobody in the house to help. If Jack didn't get medical assistance immediately, Langdon Carmichael would die. If he called the police or the paramedics, his own ass would be grass. What was he doing there, breaking into a billionaire's home in the dead of night? No, Jack couldn't possibly summon help. He had to get out while he still had time.

Hey, if the guy wanted to die, if he went to all this trouble to die, let him die, right? Who was Jack Lucas to interfere with another man's wishes? He grabbed up the chalice and ran out of the library, panicked. But he knew he was doing the wrong thing. Life was too precious to waste. A man in despair one day can be happy the next. He had to save Langdon Carmichael's life.

Jack came to a halt in the large vestibule leading to the front door. The main door must certainly be wired for the night, to open it would be to set off the alarm. He turned away; he'd have to go out the way he came, by the roof. Wait, no! *If he opened the front door, the alarm would go off, and the police would come.* If the police came, Langdon Carmichael might be found in time.

Jack looked around; there had to be evidence of the alarm somewhere. Yeah, there it was, down by the baseboard a couple of inches above the floor. Two crossed electric eye beams, focused on the door. Anybody walking through them would trigger the alarm. He stood up, tucking the precious chalice firmly under his arm. Then he opened the front door and walked out.

Hell broke loose, a loud shrieking of electronic sirens. Jack broke into a run, dashing around the corner of Fifth Avenue and east on Seventy-fourth Street. On Lexington Avenue, he came to a halt, three blocks away from Langdon Carmichael's armory.

He was safe, and he'd gotten away with it. Sir Jack Lucas Galahad, whose strength was as the strength of ten because his heart was pure, had finally achieved the Holy Grail.

The ward was dark and silent; everyone in the mental hospital was asleep. Jack came in quietly and waked to the foot of Parry's bed.

"Wake up," he said. He took Langdon Carmichael's loving cup and put it into Parry's lifeless hands, bringing the hands up and wrapping them around the Grail, which now rested on Parry's chest.

"I did my side of the bargain. Are you gonna wake up now?" He looked down at Parry, who didn't move a muscle. "You want to think about it a little more?" Jack asked gently. "Okay, take your time."

As for Jack, he was totally beat. He couldn't keep his eyes open. Every muscle he owned ached, along with a few he didn't know he had. He pulled a chair up to the bed, settled himself into it, put his cowboy-booted feet up on Parry's blanket, and fell fast asleep.

* * *

Light began to trickle in through the large windows of the hospital ward from the breaking dawn outside. The patients still slept. Jack Lucas still slept. Parry opened his eyes.

He lay on his back, looking up at the shadows still gathered on the ceiling. He had no idea where he was or why he was there. He didn't know what day it was, or what year. But there was something in his hands . . . something cold, heavy, metal, silver . . . he felt it, touching it all over. Looking down, Parry saw with an enormous surge of joy what he was holding. It was the Holy Grail, the only thing that could cure the incurable wound.

Close by the bed, crumpled uncomfortably in a chair, was Jack, and Parry knew it was Jack who had brought him the Grail. He'd been right; the Little People had been right. Jack Lucas was the One. Parry smiled happily.

"I had this dream, Jack," he whispered in a tone of wonder. "I was married. I was married to this beautiful woman. . . . And you were there, too."

Jack opened his eyes, but didn't move or speak. "I really miss her, Jack," Parry whispered. "Is that okay? Can I miss her now?" Tears formed in Jack's eyes, but he didn't turn around. He knew what Parry was really saying. He understood that Parry was asking, is it safe to think about Elizabeth? Can I put her into the past without going mad? Is it the knightly thing to do?

Jack didn't reply; he couldn't, he was too choked up to speak. But somehow Parry must have gotten the message. "Thank you," he whispered. And both of them fell asleep again, this time not to dream.

Lydia Sinclair got off the bus in front of the Oakbrook Institute. She was carrying today's newspaper, with its lead story about the miraculous recovery of

Langdon Carmichael, whose suicide had been interrupted by a botched and bungled burglary. The burglar had gotten away empty-handed, but the billionaire would live. She also carried a fresh bunch of flowers and some lovely new towels she'd picked up at Macy's white sale. They'd go very nicely with Parry's sheets. As soon as she walked into the ward she knew something was different. Parry wasn't in his bed. The bed was empty. Lydia's face blanched, and the breath caught in her throat. Where was he?

Oh, my God, there he was, up out of bed and leading the other patients in his favorite song. *He was out of bed!* Lydia gasped, and let the packages fall from her fingers.

Parry turned and saw her, and his face lit up like Christmas. ''Hiya, sweetheart! Where ya been?'' he called.

She tried to speak, but no words would come. Instead, tears fell hotly from her eyes, yet she smiled at him while she was weeping.

''Hey, what's that face all about?'' Parry asked, coming up to Lydia and wrapping his arms around her. ''Hey, why are you crying? Don't cry . . . hey!''

Lydia threw her arms around his neck and bawled for sheer gladness while Parry held her lovingly. ''Are you my girl?'' he asked her gently, patting her back like you do to a baby. ''Are you my girl?''

Lydia sobbed and nodded yes, clinging to Parry as tightly as she could. Parry hugged back; Jack had never seen him so happy.

Jack slipped by them unnoticed. They didn't need him right now; they didn't need anybody but each other. He'd come back tomorrow.

Meanwhile, there was something important he still had to do. Compared with it, stealing the Holy Grail was a snap.

* * *

The Video Spot wasn't busy, and Anne Napolitano had taken a few minutes to go into her private office and go over the week's receipts. When she heard the knock on the door, she called out a grudging "Yeah," without looking up. It was only when the door opened and closed and nobody said anything that Anne raised her head from her accounts. Jack Lucas was standing there looking at her. In his hand was a bouquet of flowers. She hadn't laid eyes on him or heard a word from him for six months, and now here he was, bigger than life and looking good, and saying nothing. Just standing there looking at her.

Anne was so shocked that for one long moment she couldn't find the breath to speak. Then, when she did speak, she was both angry and unnerved. "Well, what do you expect me to do, applaud?" Her cheeks and neck were flushed a dull red with emotion.

Jack didn't answer, but he was looking pretty sheepish.

"What? What?" Anne challenged. "What did you come here for? Did you come to get the rest of your stuff? There's no more stuff. It all got burned . . . accidentally. Jack, don't do this," she warned. His continued silence was making her crazy. "Whatever the hell you're doing, don't do this, okay? You don't just show up here out of nowhere and then just stand there like a statue and make me do all the work. What did you come here for?"

Jack drew in a deep breath. "I . . . uh . . . I love you," he said at last, barely audible.

"What?" Anne stood up slowly and came from around her desk. Jack backed up in fear, until his back was against the wall of porno tapes, and he had no more room to maneuver.

"I didn't get all that," Anne growled. "Would you run that by me again?"

Jack was sweating bullets here. This was the hardest thing he had ever had to do in his life. He knew what a shit he'd been, and how much he owed Anne, and he knew that Anne wasn't going to make things easy for him. Life with her would be one very long and loud battle. But what the hell? Everybody had a cross to bear in this life and Anne Napolitano's Italian temper would be Jack's cross. If he got over this first hurdle.

"I . . . uh . . . I think . . . uh, I *realize* I love you," and he sighed deeply.

Anne's brows drew together and fire flashed from her jet-black eyes. "You love me? *You love me?* You son . . . of . . . a . . . bitch!" Hauling off, she gave Jack a real crack across the jowls, hard enough to stun an ox. Jack saw stars and heard bells; his knees buckled and he began to slip to the floor.

Anne was on him in an instant, her lips on his, devouring him with her passion, tugging at the buttons and zippers of his clothes. Jack Lucas was too weak to protest, too weak to stand up, too weak to struggle, but not too weak to make crazy love, the best lovemaking of his life, with his woman.

"God, what a beautiful night," said Parry, deeply moved by the moon, and the park, and the joy of being alive.

"Yeah," Jack agreed. He looked up at the clouds that had gathered over the face of the moon. Through the silver moonlight, he could see them moving. "Hey . . . am I doing that?" he asked.

"You know it," Parry assured him.

The two friends lay side by side on the Sheep Meadow, cloudbusting, at peace with the world, just watching the cloud formations scud across the face of the moon.

And oh, yeah, one more thing. Both of them were naked.